Away from Home

The success of Gary and Kevin's team, Bank Vale United, leads to an invitation to make a sponsored tour during the holidays to play other school teams. The unaccustomed freedom, away from home surroundings, provokes lively reaction from the players and provides some exciting ingredients in this third in the series of books about Bank Vale United.

Also by Michael Hardcastle

Football Stories

Soccer Special
Free Kick
Half a Team
Mascot
The Team That Wouldn't Give In
United!

Motocross Stories

Fast From the Gate
The Green Machine
Roar to Victory
Tiger of the Track

Riding Stories

The Saturday Horse
The Switch Horse
Winning Rider

Caught Out (A Cricket Story)
Rival Games (An Athletics Story)
The Shooters (A Netball Story)

Michael Hardcastle regularly visits schools and libraries around
the country. If you would like to meet him, please ask your
teacher or librarian to write to the address below:

> MAMMOTH Press Office
> 38 Hans Crescent
> London SW1X 0LZ

MICHAEL HARDCASTLE

Away from Home

MAMMOTH

First published in Great Britain 1974
by Methuen Children's Books Ltd
Methuen paperback edition published 1974
Published 1990 by Mammoth
an imprint of Mandarin Paperbacks
Michelin House, 81 Fulham Road, London SW3 6RB
Reprinted 1991

Mandarin is an imprint of the Octopus Publishing Group

Text copyright © 1974 Michael Hardcastle
Illustrations copyright © 1974 Methuen Children's Books Ltd

Illustrated by Trevor Stubley
ISBN 0 7497 0479 9

A CIP catalogue record for this title
is available from the British Library

Printed in Great Britain
by Cox & Wyman Ltd, Reading, Berkshire

One

Keith Nash rushed in absolutely bursting with the news that he'd been invited to go on tour. It was the best thing that had happened to him in the whole of his life. It was as good as being a professional footballer already. It was something he had day-dreamed about for weeks—and now it was all coming true.

"It's a change for you to be home early, Keith," said his mother, who was preparing tea in the kitchen. "Didn't anyone want to play football with you after school."

"No—I mean—yes. I mean, something better than that's happened. You see, it's just—"

"*Better* than playing football!" Mrs Nash remarked, raising her eyebrows in mock amazement. "You do astonish me, Keith. I never thought I'd hear *you* say that anything could be better than football. There's hope for you yet. So it's as well I've got something in so that we

5

can celebrate. Look, strawberries."

"Oh, yes, great," Keith replied with a marked lack of enthusiasm. He was beginning to be a bit confused about how he should explain what had happened. His mother wasn't usually dim but she just didn't seem to understand what he was talking about. He tried again.

"You see, we didn't play football this after-noon because, well, because—"

"Look, you can have a strawberry now, if you like, because tea won't be ready for a few minutes yet. I just didn't expect you to be in so soon."

She offered him the bowl and automatically he chose the largest. After one bite, he swallowed it. This time Mrs Nash's astonishment was quite genuine.

"And there was I thinking that you'd enjoy every mouthful of those strawberries," she said. "After all, you did say they were your favourite fruit. Keith, you haven't been getting into trouble, have you?"

"Look, Mum, can I explain—please?" He swal-lowed hard and to his relief she didn't interrupt. She leaned back against the draining-board and folded her arms. His confidence returned when he realized that she really was going to listen to him this time.

"Well, after lunch the Headmaster sent for me. I guessed what it could be but I was a bit scared in case I was wrong. But I was right. It was great, just great! Mum, I've been selected to go on tour with the Town Boys' soccer team the week after school finishes. Oh, and I've also been picked as vice-captain. How about that?"

"How about that indeed," Mrs Nash replied, smiling at Keith's obvious delight in telling her the news. "Well, that certainly is something, Keith. Congratulations!"

"Thanks, Mum," Keith said modestly. "I knew you'd be pleased. I mean, you've always been keen on hearing about United, haven't you?"

Bank Vale United was the team Keith captained in the Sunday Junior League—a team that had played with a lot of success in the two seasons of its existence even though it hadn't yet won the Cup or the Championship. It was true that Mrs Nash always had taken an interest in the players and their matches although she still insisted that Keith accompany her to chapel on Sunday mornings when he would have preferred to spend the time training or working out tactics for the match in the afternoon.

"Have any of the other United players been

selected for this tour?" she wanted to know.

"Yes, that's one of the great things about it. Kevin Ripley and Gary Ansell have been picked as well. You see, it's made up of boys from several schools in the town. I'm the only one from Bankside, though. We're going to play three matches in three different towns and stay overnight in each of them. And we've got our own motor-coach, too. I'll bet it's just like the one Albion use when they go off to their away matches in the First Division. And—"

"And who's paying for this tour?" Keith's mother asked. Her smile had suddenly been replaced by a frown. Keith crossed his fingers in case she started raising difficulties.

"Oh, that's all been fixed up," he assured her. "The Education Department, or the Sports Council, or somebody like that are paying for all the expenses of travelling and hotels and things like that. But, er, well, the Head said we'd probably need some extra pocket money—you know."

"The *Head* said that?" Mrs Nash asked unbelievingly.

"Er, well, something like that, Mum. But he said parents wouldn't have to bear the cost because the tour was educational—we'd be young

ambassadors for the town. I didn't quite get that."

"I expect he meant that you'll be representing the town officially when you go to these other places. If you're called the Town Boys' team then people will think of the town and judge it by your conduct."

Keith nodded vigorously. "Yes, that's it—that's what the Head said—sort of. He said it's an honour for me and the school. I nearly asked him for a half-holiday for being selected, but I don't expect he'd have given me one because term ends next week."

"Do you know most of the other boys who are going on the tour? How many are going."

"Fourteen or fifteen—I don't think they've decided about one player yet. I know nearly all of them, actually. We all took part in that trial match last week, you know. I told you I had a good game—and I even scored a goal. That's not bad for someone who's usually a defensive wing-half—that's what Mr Gregsten said I was. I don't think I completely agree with him. It depends how the game's going as to how I play."

"Is Mr Gregsten going with you? Didn't you say he was a sports master?"

"I think he's described as a sports adviser—something like that. Yes, he's going."

"Do I know any of the other boys, apart from Kevin and Gary?"

Keith wrinkled his nose. "Nick Abel-Smith's been picked," he admitted in a low voice.

"Oh, isn't he the boy who used to play for United—the one you fell out with? Yes, I remember. You all clubbed together to raise money to pay his transfer fee. But then there was some trouble, and you all fell out."

"He *is* a trouble-maker," Keith said emphatically. "But he won't be able to run things his way on this tour. He won't be the best player this time. And I'm the official vice-captain, anyway, so he'll have to do what the captain and I say."

"And who's the captain?"

"Crispin Jones. He's great, though he doesn't even look like a footballer. He looks like a swot. He even wears specs."

"And is he—a swot, I mean?"

Keith nodded. "Yeah, he's a bit brainy, is Crispy. But he can play a bit, too. Anywhere, really, though he likes to dazzle 'em on the left wing.

"Hey," he rushed on, "can I go round to see Kevin and Gary? We can start working out a few moves to beat the opposition. We'll be up against some good sides, I expect."

"After tea," she replied. "If you go out now you'll not be back for hours. I know you when you start talking about football with those two. You never know when to stop."

Keith didn't feel he could object to the delay. After all, the important thing was that he was going on tour.

He slowed down when he reached the strawberries-and-cream stage. It was true that he liked them better than any other food; so, although he kept glancing at his watch, he took his time over finishing them. Then he thought he'd better offer to help with the washing-up. With the matter of the pocket money for the tour still to be decided he wanted to stay in his mother's good books.

"No, it's all right, love, you can go out now and celebrate the good news with Kevin and Gary," she said to his great delight. "But don't be late in. You've still got to go to school tomorrow."

Keith was at the front gate in under twenty seconds and he would have run all the way to Gary's home if he hadn't met Gary coming in the opposite direction on his way to see him.

They greeted each other like conquering heroes or men who've just scored the winning goal in a Wembley Cup Final. Both arms held high, fists clenched to punch the air, they yelled the same word at each other ... "Grrr-eat!" Then they slapped each other on the back and danced what was almost a jig.

Automatically, they turned together to walk towards Kevin's home. They were soon so deep in conversation about the prospects for the tour that they'd hardly have noticed if Dave Archer, Albion's brilliant right-winger and their footballing hero, had passed within a few paces of them.

Both knew by name all the other members of the touring party, though they knew the play of some of them better than others. Nick Abel-Smith and Crispin Jones were the two they talked about most. Although Nick had been their team-mate with United for only a brief spell it was an unforgettable experience. Neither of them was keen on the idea of playing alongside him again.

"I think Smithy's lucky to be chosen because he didn't play so well in the trial," Gary observed. "You almost played him out of the game, Keith," he added, much to his friend's satisfaction.

"Kevin's playing some great stuff these days,"

Gary went on, "so I reckon he's sure to be in the team for the first match. Crispin Jones will be on the left wing with me on the right so that only leaves two places to fill—and there are two centre-forwards in the party. So Smithy will be *very* lucky if he gets a game."

Keith nodded his agreement. He'd been thinking exactly the same. As vice-captain, he himself was certain of his place. But he was just a bit doubtful whether Gary himself was a certainty to play in the opening game. There were other forwards who might be chosen for the right-wing position. It wasn't the moment to mention that, however. Gary was easily upset when he thought his football skills were being questioned—even when they weren't.

By now they were quite close to where Kevin lived and Gary remarked that it was surprising they couldn't hear United's inside-right. Kevin was always exuberant and noisy when he had something to celebrate—such as a goal (even a very simple goal that anyone could have netted) —so tonight he should be in top form. Yet there wasn't a sound to be heard from the house as they walked up the garden path.

"He must have gone out looking for us," Keith suggested. He was sure that was the case when he saw that Kevin's father was coming to the door in answer to their ring.

Mr Ripley was tall and thin with a pointed black beard and he didn't seem very pleased to see them.

"You'll be wanting Kevin, I expect," he said before they could speak a word. "Well, he's not here. His mother rushed him off to hospital and now he's on the way to see our doctor. How long they'll be there I've no idea, but he won't be going out of this house again tonight. You can bank on that."

"Gosh," said Gary, his eyes widening in amazement and worry, "what's happened to him, Mr Ripley?"

"Exactly what I said would happen to him if he went on acting like a prize idiot. He came rushing home like a mad thing, shouting his head off that he was going off on some football outing or other. Before we could get any sense out of him he flew out of the back door and started swinging on the apple tree. If I've told him once I've told him a hundred times, no tree will stand up to that sort of treatment for ever.

"That branch was so weakened by all his swinging that it broke. Naturally, it was bound to, one of these days. Anyway, as he was falling

Kevin tried to save himself by grabbing at another branch with his right hand. He managed that, but the strain on his hand damaged the ligaments. Probably even tore them, I shouldn't wonder. He was in so much pain we had to take him to hospital, or rather, his mother took him. She's just rung me to say he can come home. But they've gone to see the doctor—our own doctor —first."

"Gosh," Gary said again, "that's terrible, Mr Ripley. Do you think he'll still be able to play football? I mean—"

"That's all you boys think of, isn't it?" Kevin's father snapped. "Football, football, football. Nothing else matters, does it? But there's more to life than football. As you'll find out, one day. Well, now that you've got the full story perhaps I can have a bit of peace. No doubt Kevin himself will fill you in on all the rest of the grisly details when next you see him."

It was obvious that Mr Ripley wasn't going to say any more; the front door was half-closed already. So, after thanking him, the boys turned away and walked slowly down the path.

They hadn't even reached the gate when Gary said, "Looks like old Kevin won't be going on this tour then. That's rotten luck—and for me as well. It'll mean that Nick Smithy will be at inside-right, and I'll *never* get a pass from him. That's not going to do my football career any good."

Two

The motor-coach taking the Town Boys' team on tour was parked near the Town Hall. It was, Mr Gregsten pointed out to the players, a very appropriate starting-off point. They were all representing their home town on this trip and they shouldn't forget that for a single moment while they were away. He promised he'd have further words to say on that subject when they reached Bonchester, the first town they were to visit.

The first arrivals chose the seats right at the back of the coach. For one thing, they guessed that Mr Gregsten would probably sit at the front near the driver. They were delighted to find that it was a much better coach than any of them had ever ridden in previously. It was even equipped with small tables, set between pairs of double seats, in the style of railway carriages.

The driver was waiting outside to stow their

luggage away in a huge compartment under the seats. But nearly every boy had something to take inside with him : bottles of Coke and fizzy orange; comics; fruit; a spare football or two; football magazines; chocolate and sweets; and, in the case of Lester Rowan, something quite mysterious which was wrapped up in a raincoat.

Lester was handling it as carefully as if it was a time-bomb. He chose a double seat in the centre of the coach and placed the box on the inside seat nearer the window. One or two of the early arrivals came up to him, wanting to know what the parcel contained.

"Oh, just something I don't want to lose," Lester replied as dismissively as possible. "It wouldn't interest you at all."

That was quite the wrong thing to say. He had made it seem very interesting indeed. Some of the boys persisted with inquiries but Lester would tell them nothing. More as a joke than anything else, Robert Tranfield made a grab at it. But, as one of the team's goalkeepers, Lester was used to keeping things out of the reach of centre-forwards. He snatched the parcel up and held it above his head and well away from Robert's clutches.

"Lay off, Tranfield, unless you want a thump

on the nose," Lester said warningly. Robert was well aware how effectively Lester could punch a ball so he wasn't going to risk a broken nose even though he himself was one of the biggest boys in the team and could usually take care of himself in any scrap.

"Keep it then, Rowan," he said airily as he strolled back to his seat. "But we'll find out sometime what you're hiding in that old coat."

Keith and Gary were already on the coach and sharing a table with Damian Cooke, a centre-half with Beltisham Wanderers, one of the teams

United played in the Sunday Junior League. They were glued to the window, anxiously awaiting the arrival of Kevin Ripley.

Until Kevin actually put in an appearance, they couldn't be certain that he would be going on the tour. His injured hand was healing well enough—as he had demonstrated to them at school before term finished—but his parents kept raising objections to the idea of him going on a football outing, as they described it. Kevin was doing all in his power to persuade them that the tour would be good for him but he wasn't sure that he was succeeding.

The previous evening, when the three boys had met on the Common for football practice, the matter was still undecided. Kevin had been in very low spirits; he almost seemed to have given up the battle as lost.

"It's very perplexing, very perplexing indeed," he'd kept muttering. "Perplexing" was his favourite word of the moment. He used it on every possible occasion whether it fitted or not. "They used to be quite interested in my football."

"Perhaps you described your brilliant goals to them too many times and they got bored," Gary suggested with a grin. Kevin didn't appreciate that remark. "That's not funny, Ansell," he snapped back. "I've scored more brilliant goals in one match than you've scored in all your miserable life. Like that goal I got against Beltisham in the last League match. That one I hit like a bullet from the edge of the penalty area after perplexing their sweeper. I made it out of—"

"See what I mean?" Gary said, appealing to Keith. "And *we've* heard it all before, dozens of times."

But, for all their jokes about each other, they were desperately keen to have Kevin on the tour with them. Things just wouldn't be the same without him. His energy and enthusiasm were great assets to a team; he sometimes used some very crafty tactics in trying to beat the opposition and never missed an opportunity to appeal for a free kick or a penalty. Nobody so enjoyed scoring a goal as he did. He'd had his troubles with United —and they with him—but the side always missed him when he was absent for any reason.

"It would be the rottenest trick anyone could do if they prevented Kevin from coming on the tour," Keith remarked as they scanned the horizon for sight of him.

"I'd rather play with him than against him," Damian Cooke admitted. Like Lester Rowan and Robert Tranfield, Damian was tall and well-built

22

for his age and he wasn't afraid of any forward. But he'd been outwitted by Kevin more than once.

Keith was just running his fingers through his short, fair hair when he suddenly jumped to his feet and whooped with delight.

"He's made it!" he yelled. "There's Kevin now."

He was racing down the narrow road alongside the Town Hall, swinging his case round and round in his left hand. Every few strides he jumped into the air with sheer exuberance. Then he skidded to a halt just a few paces away from the coach. By now, of course, everyone on the bus was aware of his arrival.

Kevin was equally aware that they were all watching him. He put his case down on the ground, raised both arms and began to punch the air rhythmically from his shoulders as he yelled at the top of his voice:

"We are the greatest, we are the greatest!"

The boys already on the bus didn't need any invitation to join in. So, for the next few seconds, chorus after chorus of "We are the greatest" rang out across the Town Hall Square. Passers-by looked up in amazement but no one seemed to object.

23

It was Mr Gregsten who had to call a halt to the team's musical endeavours. He held up a hand and then moved to the open door to signal to Kevin to come aboard.

"I'm glad to hear you're in such good spirits, lads," he told them with a smile as he welcomed Kevin with a pat on the shoulder. "I hope we'll all still be in such good spirits after the first match of the tour this afternoon. When we're all settled down and the journey's begun I'll announce the

team. I expect that's what you're all waiting to hear."

"Hope I'm playing," Kevin said as he flung himself into the seat beside Keith. "Don't see how the team can have any hope of winning today if I'm not playing."

"We didn't even think you were coming," Keith remarked. "I thought your folks were going to keep you at home."

"They'd've had to lock me in, then," Kevin replied aggressively. "If they'd tried that I'd still have broken out by smashing a window. I'd got all my plans ready to disappear during the night. I wasn't going to miss this tour for anything. I won't care if I don't get a game—though, of course, they'll just have to put me in the side to make sure we win."

"What made them change their mind, Kevin?" Gary asked.

Kevin shook his head, and then shrugged his shoulders for good measure. "Don't know," he admitted. "It's very perplexing. Right up to the time I went to bed they were still saying 'No'. Then they just said I could go—but if I got into any trouble they'd never let me play football again. Not even for United."

"Gosh," Gary breathed, quite shattered by that

26

thought; that was the worst punishment anybody could hand out to a boy like Kevin (or to Gary himself, come to that).

"Parents are funny people," Kevin remarked. "You never know where you are with them or what they're going to do next. *Very* perplexing."

By now all the other members of the team had arrived and sorted out their seating arrangements. The coach was big enough for each boy to have a double seat to himself if he'd wanted it but they'd all split into groups to be with their friends. All, that is, except Crispin Jones who was already involved in a deep conversation with Mr Gregsten about tactics for the first match. They were also discussing the composition of the team and they wanted no one to overhear what was being said.

Both Mr Gregsten, who now described himself as the Manager of the team, and Crispin, the captain, knew that the boys who were left out were going to be very disappointed, even though they'd get a game later. But the first team to be selected would obviously be the *best* team and all the boys would realize that. So it had to be chosen with great care.

They had plenty of time to make up their minds. Bonchester was more than a hundred miles away and so wouldn't be reached until the middle of the afternoon (the kick-off had been fixed for 4.30 p.m.). Before that the party would be stopping for lunch at a cafe near the motorway they'd be crossing. But, Mr Gregsten had already pointed out, it wasn't going to be a huge meal.

"Professional players only have a very light meal just before a game—so that's what we're going to do. We'll have our main meal of the day this evening with the Bonchester Boys. So don't stuff yourself with lemonade and biscuits and sweets on the journey. If I see that any boy is unfit through over-eating he certainly won't be playing for our team."

After the initial excitement of starting the journey and waving to people as the coach made its way through the town they gradually settled down to chat, to play cards or, in a few cases, to read books or comics. Each one was also looking forward to—and yet secretly dreading—the moment when the Manager would reveal which players would be turning out against Bonchester. Only Crispin and Keith could be confident that they would be in the side.

Crispin took his duties as captain and co-selector seriously, as seriously as he took most things. Yet he had a good sense of humour which (though only occasionally) he displayed on the soccer field. When he was in his most brilliant form he sometimes tried some exhibition stuff just for the fun of fooling opponents: pretending to have lost the ball and then suddenly flicking it upwards on his instep, lobbing it over his head, spinning round to trap it again and then darting off in the direction he was least expected to take. Another ruse he would try was the one where he would beat a defender by slipping the ball through his legs and sprinting round him before the boy could recover.

Slimly-built with plenty of long, straight, dark hair, he always wore spectacles when he wasn't actually playing—and sometimes he took his glasses with him on to the pitch and dismayed opponents by putting them on briefly when he was about to receive a pass.

Referees rarely appreciated that sort of comedy and Crispin had been cautioned by them for indulging in "ungentlemanly conduct". He always apologised so earnestly that he was quickly forgiven but he could seldom be restrained from taking the mickey out of the opposition in other ways. His style of play was deceptive. Because he didn't waste time or effort in running about a lot he seemed to be doing very little. Yet whenever he had possession it was practically impossible for one opponent on his own to take the ball off him.

When Crispin passed the ball it invariably went precisely where he intended it to go. Moreover, the team-mate who received it was always the one in the best position to make use of the ball. But if that player then made a hash of the movement Crispin would let him know about it in a few well-chosen words.

When he wasn't playing or talking about football Crispin usually buried himself in a book. His reading covered an astonishing range of subjects and appeared to follow no set pattern. Volumes on astrology and smuggling, biographies of explorers and famous soldiers, and even guide books to faraway places, would be devoured in rapid succession. If he stated that something was a fact he was not often challenged; he had the annoying habit of nearly always being right. Small wonder that his school-mates, and several of his team-mates referred to him as "The Professor". Crispin accepted that as a tribute he thoroughly deserved.

His discussion with Mr Gregsten about the team for the first match of the tour was now almost at an end. The only point on which they had disagreed concerned the position of centre-forward. Crispin was all for playing Kevin Ripley in spite of his injured hand.

"That doesn't affect his footwork, does it?" Crispin remarked with what he considered to be irrefutable logic.

"True," the Manager conceded, "but I think Ripley needs just a little more time to get over his accident."

He went on, "Besides, Tranfield is the better player in the air. His heading ability has improved a lot just lately. Also, I think he plays better in partnership with Abel-Smith. I suspect there's a bit of rivalry between Ripley and Abel-Smith, each trying to out-do the other in producing the clever stuff."

Crispin didn't give in easily, if at all. "Yes, but we'll be playing it on the ground, not in the air. And Ripley can use *both* feet, not just the right— which is what Tranfield does most of the time."

Mr Gregsten nodded. "Yes, that's a fair comment, Crispin. But if we give Ripley that extra day to recover he'll be doubly keen to do well in the second match of the tour—if only to keep his place for the last match. In any case, we don't want Bonchester to think we're playing a bunch of hospital patients, and that's what they would think if we played a bandaged centre-forward.

They'd be sure to give Ripley a rough time in those circumstances. In my experience boys are just as likely to try and take advantage of an injury as any of the professional teams."

"Ah, but Ripley wouldn't let 'em. He'd dish out as much as he got," Crispin countered. "More, probably, if I know Kevin."

"Yes, well, we don't want to start a war during the opening match so I think we'll settle for Tranfield to lead the attack," Mr Gregsten said.

Crispin gave in gracefully. "You're the boss, Mr Gregsten," he replied—and looked sideways at the Manager over his spectacles to see how he'd take the comment. But the Manager just smiled. He enjoyed his conversations with Crispin.

When Mr Gregsten stood up and moved a few paces down the aisle the hum of conversation stopped immediately. Coke bottles were lowered, cards and comics were abandoned. Every player waited expectantly for the vital news announcement. To each of them, being chosen to play in the Bonchester match was as important as winning a place in the England team.

"Right, lads, your first ordeal is over," he began. "I know that waiting is always worse than anything else. But it's not easy to choose a team of eleven when you have fifteen players of equal

brilliance."

He thought there might have been some reaction to that—if only in the form of ironic cheers—but not a mouth opened, not a muscle moved. He'd never faced such an attentive audience in his entire career.

"Okay, then," he continued with a grin, "let's end the suspense. This is the team: in goal, Lester Rowan; full-backs, Gavin Streeter and Graham Connally; half-backs, Keith Nash, Damian Cooke and Jonathan Castree; forwards, Gary

33

Ansell, Nick Abel-Smith, Robert Tranfield, Adrian Dawnay and, finally, your captain himself, Crispin Jones.

"Well, that's it. As I've said before, the *next* match you play is always the important one. So the second match of the tour will be just as important as the first.

"Those boys who aren't playing in the first game will probably play in the second, so there's nothing to be disappointed about in missing today's game—nothing at all. In any case, two of you will be substitutes, so you might get a bit of action after all."

Mr Gregsten added that they'd be stopping in half-an-hour for lunch and he'd have a few more words to say about tactics for the match. He tried to remind them about the perils of over-eating but by the time he reached that point none of the boys was really listening to a word he said. Each of them was reacting in his own way to the news they'd just been given.

Lester Rowan, for instance, was thinking more about his mysterious box than about football. He'd expected to be chosen for the first game and that meant that he'd have to make some arrangements to safeguard the box. Of course, he could take it into goal with him and leave it in a corner of the net. But that really was a bit risky because if he let in a goal the ball might hit the box and damage the contents.

So far only Robert Tranfield had made any move to snatch the box and Lester was thankful that Tranfield was also playing in this afternoon's match and so would have his mind on other things. On the other hand, Tranfield might get one of his pals to have a go at pinching the box. So Lester would have to think very carefully about the best way of protecting his most precious possession.

Gary Ansell hadn't really been very sure about whether he'd be picked for the opening match, even though he wouldn't have admitted that doubt to anyone. He was so relieved to know he was in the side that he couldn't help murmuring "Great!" as he glanced across at Keith. But he also caught the eye of Kevin so he hastily added: "Bad luck, Kevin. But you'll be in the next match —and then we can join up in our great partnership again. We'll show 'em we're the best right-wing pair in football."

Kevin just nodded. He was bitterly disappointed at being left out but at least he had a good excuse. "Gregsten couldn't consider me for a place because of my injury," he explained to his pals. Because they were in the team they could afford to be sympathetic. So they smiled carefully and nodded agreement with everything he said. Continued Kevin: "He doesn't realize yet that I'm fully recovered. But if I come on as sub I'll be able to show him. Anyway, he'll need me for the second match, because this forward line isn't good enough without me in it. It'll be perplexing if they can score plenty of goals without my help."

Nick Abel-Smith's thin face and dark, brooding eyes showed neither surprise nor pleasure at his selection. Like Lester Rowan, he had simply expected to be playing. All the same, he was glad that Kevin had been omitted. Not so long ago they had been good friends; now they were deadly rivals.

For his part, Crispin Jones wasn't thinking about any of his team-mates, or the forthcoming match, or even about football. Already he had resumed reading his book on the subject of famous escapes from prison. It was so interesting that he didn't realize that the coach had stopped outside the cafe where they were to have lunch. When Mr Gregsten said, "Come *on*, Crispin, we're there," he just nodded, stuck the book under his arm and followed the rest of the players out of the coach.

Three

There was just half-an-hour to go to the kick-off when the Town Boys arrived at the Bonchester football ground. Already a sprinkling of spectators was present and all of them would be cheering for the home team. The ground itself was luxurious compared to most of the ones the Town Boys had played on in the past. There were changing-rooms and showers for each team and the referee had a room to himself. In spite of the fact that it was mid-summer, and the pitch had been in use all winter, there was plenty of grass on it and the goal posts gleamed with fresh white paint.

"Well, we can't blame the pitch if we lose," Mr Gregsten joked. Immediately, half the team yelled back at him: "We aren't going to lose! We'll win by at least three goals."

Mr Gregsten nodded approvingly. "That's the spirit, lads. Just make sure the town is proud of the way we play as well as pleased with the result. I'll be phoning a report to our local paper tonight so everyone at home will know tomorrow how we got on."

That thrilled the players more than anything. All the forwards were thinking that if they scored their own names would also be in the newspaper report. That would really impress their friends at home. The paper would also be read by the officials at Albion, their local First Division club, and they'd probably want to check up on the goal-scorers when they returned home. And that could lead to a full-time career in football when they were a bit older.

As the boys moved off into their dressing-room their Manager fell into conversation with Mr Andrews, who was in charge of the Bonchester side. The players had been hoping to have a glimpse of the opposition ("so we can size them up," as Keith put it) but for some reason they were keeping out of sight.

The four boys who were not playing in the match watched with envy as their friends changed into the brand new gear they were to use on the tour: orange shirts, with a diagonal blue stripe running from shoulder to waist, and white shorts. It was the most dazzling strip they'd ever seen and it was a proud moment when they put those shirts on for the first time. The dressing-room was furnished with a wall mirror and the players crowded round it, not merely so that they could comb their hair properly but so that they could admire themselves in the Town colours.

"Just a word before we go out, lads," Crispin said. They all paused to listen to him; apart from being their captain, he had an excellent know-ledge of tactics. If he said he wanted a game to be played in a particular way, that was usually the best way to play it.

"The other lot will attack from the beginning, I expect. Home sides always do. Their supporters expect it. They'll think we need a bit of time to settle down. But we don't. We're the better side —must be—so we're going to control the game. We're going to hit 'em hard, right from the start. If I win the toss I'll choose to kick-off. That will give us an advantage straight away. It doesn't bother us which way they choose to play, uphill or downhill.

"I expect you all to play as hard as you've ever played in your lives," he went on, adding a touch of Lord Nelson to his orders. "If anybody chickens out of a tackle or anything like that he's had it for the next match. I'll see to that, whatever Mr Gregsten says. So, remember, give it everything you've got. Town Boys are not going to get licked on this tour."

Just as he finished speaking, the referee looked in. He cast a professional eye over the players, as if trying to pinpoint any likely trouble-makers, and then told them that he wanted a clean game. All fouls, he promised, would be punished severely. Crispin told him that his team didn't commit fouls. "Glad to hear it," said the referee, and departed.

The Town Boys followed him on to the pitch. They were greeted by cheers from their four team-mates and a few gentle, and meaningless, boos from the Bonchester fans whose numbers had increased quite considerably. There had been plenty of publicity in the Town for the match and to the Town Boys it already had something of the atmosphere of a top League match or a Cup-tie.

Mr Gregsten was not the sort of man to drown his players with floods of last-minute advice. He had said all that was necessary after lunch and now he relied on them to do their best—to win if they could but, whatever the result, to play good football and to act like sportsmen. He knew

that Crispin would exercise all the control necessary on the pitch.

With Mr Andrews he watched the captains
shake hands and then toss-up. And when Crispin
chose to kick-off the two men strolled towards
their seats in the tiny grandstand above the
dressing-rooms.

To the amazement of both of them, Bonchester
had taken the lead even before they reached
those seats. For when Robert Tranfield kicked-off
by pushing the ball to Nick Abel-Smith for Nick
to hit a long pass to the left wing Crispin, quite
incredibly, failed to trap the ball. It bounced over
his up-lifted boot and into touch. The Bonchester
wing-half retrieved the ball with remarkable
speed and took a long throw-in. The ball went
straight to his centre-forward who was already
moving up-field at speed.

The centre-forward resisted Damian Cooke's
challenge with ominous ease and then switched
the ball to his winger. Graham Connally, who
always had a tendency to move up in support of
his own forwards, had to back-pedal furiously.
The winger gave him no chance at all to catch up.
He cracked the ball hard and low into the centre
—where the Town defence was already paper-
thin.

Bonchester's inside-right swept the ball further across goal; Gavin Streeter missed his kick completely; and Bonchester's centre-forward, who had never stopped running, thrust his leg out and diverted the ball into the net off the base of the far post. If he'd hit his shot properly the ball might well have gone to some area of the goal that Lester Rowan was covering. As it was, Lester had no chance at all of getting down to save at the foot of the post.

The Town Boys were completely stunned. None of them could recall ever conceding a goal as fast as that one. Crispin Jones, who had been a spectator for most of the move that led to the disaster, was for once quite speechless. After all, the first mistake had been his own. He couldn't explain why it had happened; he was sure he had the ball covered when it came to him from Nick's pass. He might have blamed his eyesight, or a bump in the pitch, but he wasn't a boy to find excuses. He'd made an error—and that was that.

Under other circumstances he would have passed a sharp comment on Damian Cooke's too hasty attempt at a tackle and Gavin Streeter's mis-kick. But at this moment he guessed they were feeling as bad about what had happened as he was himself.

Adrian Dawnay, his wing partner, who hadn't touched the ball yet, said: "Hey, that must be the fastest goal on record!" He even sounded quite pleased about it, as though Town Boys could take some of the credit for it.

"Rubbish," Crispin replied cuttingly. "When Jim Fryatt played centre-forward for Bradford he had the ball in the net in a match against Tranmere Rovers in just four seconds. Bonchester must have taken twice as long as that—*at least*." Crispin felt a lot better after producing that gem of information. Adrian looked suitably apologetic.

"Don't panic, lads, *we* haven't started yet," Crispin called to the other players.

Mr Andrews had the same feeling of jubilation as his players but he was trying hard not to show it. He risked a glance at Mr Gregsten to see how he was taking the setback. Mr Gregsten was frowning and shaking his head gently.

"I hope this isn't going to be a one-sided game that becomes a rout," Mr Andrews murmured. "That would be very embarrassing."

He didn't sound as though he'd be embarrassed, however. In fact, he now gave the impression that nothing would please him more than to see his team triumph by the widest possible margin.

"No chance of that," Mr Gregsten replied firmly. "My boys won't let that happen again. Best to get your mistakes over early, I think. Once they settle down you won't see which way they go. You'll probably be very sorry you scored so soon."

The Town Boys might have heard him, judging by the furious way they tore into the opposition when Robert Tranfield kicked-off for the second time within a minute. This time Nick wasn't risking a pass to the left-wing. Nor did he put the ball over to the right; he didn't trust Ansell not to make the same mistake as his captain. Instead, he burrowed through the middle, exercising all his talent for keeping possesssion of the ball. Only when he saw Tranfield running into a gap on his left did he release it—and then he called for a return pass.

Robert, however, felt he could take on the opposition on his own. He bulldozed into the centre-half when the latter came in for a tackle. The referee blew for a foul—which Robert hotly disputed.

"Look, you'd better not argue with me, sonny, or I'll have to send you off," the referee told him.

The official was determined to stamp his authority on the game from the outset and he wasn't going to allow any nonsense, as he put it, from anyone. Rather to his surprise, he had Crispin to support him.

"Just cool it, Tranfield," the captain ordered. "We can probably beat this lot with nine players but we might as well have eleven if we can."

Bonchester wasted the free kick because they hadn't worked out a plan to make the best use of it. Damian Cooke beat the centre-forward in the air for it and immediately felt better as he lofted a pass to the right wing. Gary Ansell came in for it immediately. He knew he wouldn't get a pass as good as this one from Abel-Smith. Quite cleverly, he dummied to go inside the full-back marking him—and then sprinted away on the outside.

"Keep going, Gary!" Kevin yelled from the touch-line. Gary didn't need any advice. He knew precisely what he was going to do. Out of the corner of his eye he had seen Robert Tranfield racing through the middle from the halfway line. His speed off the mark was one of Robert's greatest assets. But Gary had no intention of sending the ball to his centre-forward. That was too

obvious; that was what the Bonchester defenders
would expect to happen.

By now Nick Abel-Smith was on the edge of the
penalty area with his arm raised to signal that he
wanted the ball. Gary ignored him, too.

Suddenly, Gary slowed down. The full-back
shadowing him hesitated, uncertain what to do
next. Without so much as a glance round Gary
slid the ball into the open space to his left. He
knew that Keith Nash would be coming up
behind in support—as he was.

Keith took the ball away to the left—but
instead of lifting it into the penalty area he

absolutely hammered it towards the left wing where Crispin Jones was standing in isolation, hands on hips. By now the point of attack had been changed completely and the Bonchester defence didn't know whether to come out or huddle in the middle. After all, two Town attackers, Tranfield and Abel-Smith, were in the box.

Crispin made no mistake this time in controlling the ball. He rolled it forward with the studs of his boot and, apparently quite casually, began to jog towards the dead-ball line. Adrian Dawnay, who knew Crispin's style of play, moved towards him as if to offer support. Now the defence felt they had to come out—or, rather, two players came out. That suited Crispin. He dealt with the first challenge by putting the ball to one side of the box and then rounding him on the other side. The second defender faced him, wide-legged and anxious. *Exactly* what Crispin wanted: the ball was pushed sharply between the defender's heels—and again Crispin shot by to collect it again.

By now he was almost on the dead-ball line. The rest of the defence had seen enough wizardry to realize that they'd have to get the ball off Crispin immediately—or suffer severely.

The first challenger had recovered sufficiently to feel that he could try again. This time he had the support of his captain, the Bonchester right-half. Together they moved in to take the ball off Crispin. To their surprise, Crispin immediately began to retreat, backing away and pulling the ball with him.

That was really the last thing they'd expected —and Crispin knew it. Suddenly, he spun round, flicking the ball into the air as he did so. When it was at ankle height he hit it high into the air.

The ball came over the penalty area in a loop. By Crispin's own high standards it wasn't the perfect centre. It was just too far out. Nick turned and raced for it and, as it came down, he sent a back-header into the goal-mouth. Robert was on his own as the ball came to him at an awkward angle. He lunged forward, trying to hook it into the net with his right foot. He got some force behind the shot but his aim was poor. The goal-keeper should have had no chance at all of saving the shot because Robert was so close to him. But the ball struck the goalie's shoulder—and bounced high over the crossbar.

"I'd've stuck that one in before the goalie could even blink," Kevin Ripley announced to his team-mates in a very loud voice. That was probably true. A nippier player than Robert Tranfield would surely have scored from such a chance for no one had been marking him.

The person who was blinking most at that moment was Mr Andrews. In the opening moments of the match he had decided that Crispin Jones represented no threat at all to his team. Now he had seen how utterly wrong that assessment was.

Mr Andrews knew that none of his own players possessed skill of that kind. He began to fear that Bonchester might not have such an easy win after all. For his part, Mr Gregsten was smiling again.

"That's better," he had murmured as Crispin bemused the home defenders and he had been ready to applaud a goal when Tranfield fired in his shot. Had he heard Kevin Ripley's remark he would have agreed with the boy; a more agile forward would have scored in that situation. He could only hope that Tranfield would improve when he got a chance to use his heading ability.

Crispin himself took the corner but it wasn't deep enough and Bonchester's captain booted it away to safety. But the pressure on the home team wasn't lifted. For the next ten minutes or so the blue-and-orange shirts of the Town attackers darted through his defence like king-fishers. Nick Abel-Smith was determined to match Crispin's soccer artistry and he was playing with enormous zest. He was the next player to create a scoring chance and his well-judged shot from beside the penalty spot was despairingly punched out by a goalkeeper who was finding that luck was on his side—for the moment. Twice the ball was scrambled off the line when it seemed odds-on it would go over for the equalizer.

Gary Ansell was seeing very little of the ball since his well-rehearsed move with Keith Nash that had led, if indirectly, to Robert's hooked shot. Now Gary decided to come inside—and he was rather dismayed when Crispin told him to stay on his wing. Crispin knew that it was the wingers who would pull the Bonchester defence apart.

The Bonchester captain had attached himself to Crispin now to try and ensure that his opposite number didn't wreck his defence again. He was a good player but he didn't possess Crispin's tactical sense. So he hadn't realized just how dangerous Nick Abel-Smith could be. He supposed that the biggest menace came from Crispin. That was his undoing.

Nick was thoroughly enjoying his freedom

from close attention by the Bonchester defence and he was combining well with Tranfield and Adrian Dawnay, who was also being given plenty of room in which to operate. Adrian's strong point was his unselfishness. When he saw that a colleague was better placed than himself to launch an attack he gave him the ball.

With so much pressure on their defence little had been seen of the Bonchester attack for some time. Yet their forwards weren't dropping back to help out. They were still hopeful of receiving the ball, perhaps from a breakaway, and getting the chance to test the Town Boys' defence. They had scored once and they reckoned they could do it again.

It didn't occur to them to go back and fetch the ball themselves. In fact, they weren't thinking like a team at all: they were playing like a collection of individuals. Instead of sitting in the grandstand Mr Andrews should have been down on the touch-line to pass on some useful information and advice. The referee wouldn't have stopped him because this was supposed to be a friendly match.

It appeared distinctly unfriendly when, more by accident than anything else, the ball suddenly arrived in the Town half of the field. Bonchester's centre-forward and Damian Cooke competed for it and, when Damian managed to scoop it away from his opponent, the centre-forward promptly tripped him.

That was really the result of frustration but it cost his side a free kick. Damian wasted no time in placing the ball and taking the kick himself. He hit it deep into the other half of the field for Robert to demonstrate how effective he could be with his head. Robert flicked the ball sideways very neatly and Nick was on to it like a cat pouncing on a mouse.

He veered sharply towards the corner of the penalty area with Gary Ansell rushing up in the hope of receiving a pass at long last. He had good reason to expect one for the boy marking Nick had suddenly returned to duty after a spell of idleness on the other flank. The Bonchester boy was confident that Nick would have to part with the ball soon—and that it would go to Gary. So he stationed himself between the two of them.

That suited Nick very well. He'd no intention of giving Gary the ball because, he was sure, Ansell would waste it. But he was happy to have Gary act as a decoy. The rest of the Bonchester defence, too, were expecting Nick to feed one of his team-mates. While they watched Nick they also tried to keep an eye on Crispin—who was drifting in towards the other corner of the box. So, trapped in their own uncertainty, the Bonchester players waited too long to do anything positive.

Nick was moving in at a deceptive speed, changing pace constantly. He swung one leg over the ball, and then the other. Each time he did so it seemed certain he was going to pass. He didn't. In desperation a full-back at last charged towards him. Nick jinked sideways and the back went sprawling past him.

Now only the goalkeeper was directly in front of him. And the goalie, too, felt he had waited long enough. He'd been told all about the theory of narrowing the angle by advancing from his line: that way the striker would have less room for his shot. Unhappily for the Bonchester goalkeeper, he came out too far and too fast. Nick was used to dealing with that situation (he hadn't a very high opinion of goalkeepers, anyway). He dummied to go one way, dragged the ball in the opposite direction with a very neat swerve—and then calmly side-footed it into the net.

He turned away even before the ball crossed the line. There was no ecstasy on his part, no punching of the air, no arm raised—in fact, no emotion at all. He regarded goal-scoring as his job and that was all there was to it.

His colleagues, of course, were almost delirious with delight. They rushed up to congratulate Nick on scoring the equalizer they felt they'd deserved for so long. Even Gary Ansell, who'd been hoping all the time that he'd get that pass from Nick, didn't hang back. He knew Mr Gregsten was watching and he wasn't going to let it be thought that he was jealous. Only Crispin signalled his pleasure with just a wave of his hand.

Mr Andrews seemed to have an obstruction in his throat. He kept swallowing, as if trying hard to remove it. He'd been so confident his team was unbeatable and that goal in the first few moments of the match had appeared to confirm it. But he had seen enough now to know that the Town Boys had an abundance of talent.

"Good goal, that," he murmured. Mr Gregsten only just heard him but he acknowledged the tribute by remarking: "Glad you enjoyed it. The boys seem to be finding their form at last."

If the first Town goal had been rather a long time in coming the second one arrived very quickly. This time Keith Nash was the real architect. Winning the ball in a midfield tussle, he raced forward, scattering would-be tacklers rather like a threshing-machine in a field of corn. Gary Ansell, sensing that his United team-mate would soon give him a pass, began to gather speed down the right wing.

The Bonchester defenders, who'd been anticipating danger from the left, were again slow to realize what was really happening. Crispin and Nick were being marked but someone had to be allowed to run free. That someone was Gary— and when Keith steered the ball into his path Gary was determined to make the most of it.

His speed—he was one of the top sprinters over 100 metres at his school—carried him past the full-back like a racing car overtaking a coal wagon. All season he had been practising high centres and the one he put over now, from close to the dead-ball line, was one of his very best.

It was precisely the kind of cross that Robert Tranfield spent hours dreaming about. One day, from a centre like this one, he intended to head home the winning goal in a World Cup Final in Moscow or Buenos Aires. But for the moment he had to be content with a well-judged downward header to his left after soaring above the Bonchester centre-half.

The ball bounced once and as it rose again Crispin Jones, whipping in like a greyhound, crashed it into the net well beyond the goal-keeper's right-hand. No one was more astonished than the Bonchester captain. He'd been left standing by Crispin's burst of speed that had carried him into the penalty area with superb timing to make the shot.

Bonchester were defending yet again when the referee blew for half-time. When the Town Boys reached their dressing-room Mr Gregsten was there to greet them and congratulate them on their performance.

"You have," he declared sincerely, "made me proud of you. Apart from the goals, which were excellent, you've played some splendid football. The opposition haven't a clue what you're going to do next. But don't ease up—don't think the game's over yet. Bonchester have got one or two —but only one or two—useful lads in their side and they'll hit back if you give them a chance. If you can score plenty of goals today then Crowley, the next team we meet, will be worried even before that match kicks-off."

Crispin Jones was the only player who'd got a knock. He rubbed the place on his ankle where he'd been accidentally kicked. It hadn't stopped him from scoring a goal but it hurt now.

Mr Gregsten came over to him. "You all right,

Crispin?" he asked. "I'll send on a substitute for the second half if you like."

Crispin shook his head. "It'll be okay in a minute or two. He caught me right on the bone. That's why it aches a bit. Just for that, I'm going to get another goal."

His Manager nodded approvingly. "That's the spirit, Crispin. That was an absolute cracker you scored. Tranfield's doing well in the air."

Early in the second half Robert had another chance to demonstrate his heading ability. Crispin, showing no sign of his injury, won a corner on the left by hitting the ball against the body of an opponent who was blocking his progress along the dead-ball line. Defenders were now swarming round him whenever he seemed likely to get the ball and Crispin was always willing to accept a corner kick when there was no better alternative for creating a scoring opportunity.

He took the kick himself and floated the ball towards the near post. Robert, alerted by his captain to the direction of the kick, went up for the ball and turned it across the face of the goal. Damian Cooke had come into the box to add his height to the attack and he tried to reach the ball ahead of Nick. But he misjudged his jump slightly and the ball struck his cheek and spun away to the ground.

Nick and a full-back went for it but neither could control it. As it ran free several players attempted to get a boot to it. The situation was developing into a wild scramble before Robert Tranfield used his weight to push through the crowd of players and toe-end the ball into the net.

Not even Robert himself would describe it as a good goal—but it counted. That was really all that mattered. Town Boys had now set up a lead they could hardly lose unless half the team was sent off or the other half was carried off with injuries. Their superiority over Bonchester had been established beyond question and Mr Andrews had resigned himself to admitting defeat. His team, too, seemed to have given up the fight.

For the rest of the match Town Boys played at their own pace, pushing the ball about with ease and confidence; it was a warm afternoon and both sides began to tire in the final quarter. For this was a big pitch and they had used up a lot of energy in switching their attack from wing to wing and running off the ball to give the best possible support to a team-mate. It was tiredness rather than bad temper which led to the final goal.

Crispin's pace had slowed down considerably but he was still being watched as closely as a stoat watches a rabbit. For whenever he had the ball, trouble was in store for the home side's defence. Now, as he jogged into the box from the right, Bonchester's captain and another defender rushed at him. Crispin put on a spurt and tried to go between them—only to be felled as they sandwiched him. The referee blew for the foul and pointed with an outstretched finger at the penalty spot.

To their credit, the Bonchester players made no attempt at a protest. Their captain even helped Crispin to his feet and inquired whether he was all right. Crispin assured him that he was. Moreover, he was going to prove it by taking the penalty kick himself.

Nick Abel-Smith came up to offer to take the responsibility off his captain but Crispin shook his head. For one thing, he had promised himself he was going to score two goals; for another, he enjoyed taking a penalty kick.

He took his time placing the ball on the spot and wiping imaginary mud off his left boot. He was well aware that the Bonchester goalie was becoming increasingly nervous. He jigged up and down on his line until Crispin stepped back for the kick.

The Town Boys' captain came at the ball at only half-pace. His body was leaning slightly to the right and the goalkeeper anticipated that the ball would be fired to his left. So he went that way. The ball went the other way. Crispin had side-footed it into the net just inside the goalie's right-hand post. It scarcely rose above the level of the grass.

That was almost the last kick of the match. When the referee blew for full-time Town Boys had gained a victory that was even easier than the score of 4-1 suggested. Their tour had begun on a note of triumph. At that moment there was no hint at all of the trouble that lay ahead.

Four

After showering and changing back into their ordinary clothes the Town Boys' party returned to their coach for the short drive to a local youth club which had been booked for the evening. There they were going to be entertained to a meal and a film show with the Bonchester players.

The excitement of the match had not yet disappeared and several of the boys were reluctant to settle into their seats. They'd been hoping to have the evening free to explore the town or even play a seven-a-side game among themselves after tea. Mr Gregsten had said something earlier in the day about "not being late to bed" but that wasn't very popular; after all, as most of them were quick to point out, they *were* on holiday.

Robert Tranfield was one of the last to get into the coach. After scoring a goal ("the most important one of the whole match because it put us two-up," he told everyone) he was in high spirits. When he spotted Lester Rowan he pounced on him immediately.

"Right, then, Goalie, where is it?" he demanded to know. "Where's that secret old parcel of yours? What've you done with it?"

Lester was looking remarkably smug. "It's where you'll never be able to find it, Tranfield," he replied. "It's so well hidden that even an army of detectives couldn't possibly find it."

"You mean a *squad* of detectives," Robert replied. He was delighted to score that point and he tried to push Lester out of the way so that he could search under his seat. Lester grabbed his arm and they began to struggle. That made Robert think that the box *must* be hidden close at hand.

One or two other players crowded round either with the aim of joining in or to encourage the combatants. But before it could develop into anything more than a minor scuffle Mr Gregsten intervened.

"Come on, now, lads, let's settle down," he called. "You should all be in a good mood after that win, not ready to fight each other. Back to your own seat, Tranfield."

Robert gave up the struggle reluctantly. But as he moved away he muttered to Lester, "I'm warning you. We'll get that parcel off you and see what you've got hidden in it."

Lester, straightening his jacket, didn't appear at all alarmed by the threat. He was congratulating himself on having made certain that none of his team-mates would find the box, whether by accident or by searching for it. For at the moment it was in the care of the coach driver, Bob Livingstone. He had raised no objection to looking after it for the time being and he had been sworn to secrecy about the contents. To Lester's delight Mr Livingstone had said that his two young daughters had the same interest so he would do his best to see that no harm came to the box—or, rather, to what was *in* the box.

Some of the boys were ready to pile out of the coach almost before it pulled up outside the youth club building. Most of them had heeded Mr Gregsten's warning not to eat too much at the pre-match meal in the cafe and now they announced that they were starving. The Bonchester players had arrived ahead of them and were already seated at the tables nearest the serving hatch.

They needn't have worried: the food was plentiful as well as appetizing. Meat pies with chips and beans and tomatoes and huge plates of bread-and-butter; fruit jelly with bananas and cream; scones and jam and cakes; and massive urns of tea. During the meal there was very little chatter but afterwards players from both teams noisily re-played some of the highlights of the afternoon's game. They'd've been quite happy to go outside and start another match but the film show was about to begin. They had been promised films about sport and they expected that to mean football. Instead, the films showed a car rally in France and the history of a horse that won the Derby.

Some of those near to the doors slipped out with the excuse that they wanted to go to the toilet but several didn't come back—except for the cold drinks and ice-cream at the interval. After the excitement of the coach trip to another city and the match itself they were restless; only a handful were really tired. In the end, Mr Gregsten was glad to get them back into the coach for the short trip to the hotel in the centre of the city.

By now it was dark and because of a complex one-way street system Mr Livingstone, the driver, had difficulty in finding the way. Once he had to turn the coach round in a cul-de-sac that backed on to railway marshalling yards, much to the amusement of his young passengers.

At last they crossed the river and climbed the short, steep hill on which stood a cathedral. The hotel they were staying at, explained Mr Greg-sten, had once been an archbishop's palace; it was a very old and important building and he didn't want any nonsense from anyone while they were there. They had to behave themselves; and those who didn't might find themselves being sent home in disgrace.

"That must be the place," Mr Livingstone remarked as he turned the coach through a narrow archway into a courtyard. The headlights illuminated an ornamental fountain and, beyond, the twin pillars that seemed to be guarding the entrance to the old palace itself. As the boys crowded up to the windows of the coach they could see, by the light of the moon, that their hotel looked more like a castle, complete with turrets and battlements.

"Gosh," Robert Tranfield said softly, "I bet it's haunted. The Haunted Castle of Bonchester!"

Nobody found that a fanciful idea; several of his team-mates were thinking exactly the same. Nobody else dared speak for a moment. They simply gazed at the massive stone building in awe.

While Mr Gregsten went off to announce their arrival to whoever was there to welcome them Mr Livingstone busied himself getting the cases out of the locker compartment under the seats. He had plenty of voluntary helpers for no one was particularly anxious to be the first into the hotel—on his own.

When they'd collected all their belongings (and for once Robert Tranfield wasn't taking the slightest interest in what Lester Rowan was carrying) they all moved off together. Now, with light streaming out of the open door, the place appeared a little more inviting.

Mr Gregsten emerged to tell them to hurry up. It was already late, he said, and they mustn't keep Miss O'Houlihan and her staff up any longer. When, still rather reluctantly, they stepped into the entrance hall the boys found only one person there to greet them: Miss O'Houlihan. There was no sign of any staff. But Miss O'Houlihan was more than enough to be going on with, they decided.

Dressed all in black, she was white-haired, small—and plump as a chicken. Her spectacles were square-shaped and clipped to the bridge of her nose. But the most extraordinary thing about her was that she was smoking a small, black cigar.

She puffed at it as she studied them over the top of her glasses. It was almost as though she was assessing each of them, making up her mind which ones could be trusted and which could not. Standing beside her, Mr Gregsten was saying nothing at all; it was as if he, too, was simply waiting for her to give her orders.

"Well, now," she said in a surprisingly strong, almost piercing, voice, "I must tell you which rooms you are to occupy. Most of them are double rooms so you will be able to share with a friend. Just one or two are single rooms but they are close to one another so no one need feel scared at being on his own.

"This is quite a large hotel—rambling, as one historian described it—which means that if you try exploring all the different corridors and staircases you'll probably get lost. And we don't want that, do we? We don't want anybody to *disappear*."

She emphasized the last word so strongly that she made it sound quite sinister. Damian Cooke wasn't the only one who gulped as he began to imagine what it would be like to disappear *for ever* in a haunted hotel. Probably their bodies would never be found because no one would know where to start looking.

As Miss O'Houlihan explained that all the rooms had a number on the door—that the bathrooms were clearly marked—that the lights would be switched off in half-an-hour (by which time *every boy* should be fast asleep)—that she didn't want to hear *another sound* before breakfast at 8.30 a.m.—as she was saying all that one or two of them noticed for the first time a man standing in the shadow of an arched doorway at the back of the hall.

They saw that he was very tall and very thin and that he was wearing a clergyman's collar. He seemed to be watching them just as intently as Miss O'Houlihan while not wishing to be seen himself.

Keith nudged Kevin in the ribs. "Look," he whispered, "over there. There's the Archbishop himself. He must be here to keep the Devil away."

"No," Kevin said. "I'll bet he *is* the Devil—in disguise. He's just trying to fool us and he'll come out later on and try and make us disappear."

Keith giggled, quite loudly. He couldn't help it, because he'd shivered just as he was going to have a quiet laugh at Kevin's remark.

Miss O'Houlihan stopped speaking immediately. She unclipped her glasses and stared freezingly at the group of boys, trying to identify the one who had been so wicked as to giggle when she was talking to them. It was Mr Gregsten who came to her assistance.

"That's enough of that, Nash," he said crisply. "I thought you would have known how to behave. You *are* vice-captain of the team, aren't you?"

"Sorry, sir," Keith said as contritely as possible. He was thankful his mother wasn't here at the moment: she was rather keen on religious places and she most certainly wouldn't have approved of any jokes about clergymen. Keith's mother regarded parsons and ministers as highly as he regarded England footballers.

Miss O'Houlihan had now completed her lecture and was telling the boys to step forward in pairs as she listed the room numbers. They didn't need a second invitation. For all of them there was a sort of dreadful excitement at the thought of venturing upstairs in this mysterious building.

Keith and Kevin went forward together like Army recruits and were allocated Room 8. Miss O'Houlihan told them to go down the passageway to her right, up the first staircase on the left, up another winding staircase from the first floor and they would find their room clearly marked on the left.

The boys departed at the double, eager to discover what kind of room it was. It might perhaps be circular, with curtains from floor to ceiling, four-poster beds—and a secret entrance at the side of a huge fireplace. But for the moment that was only guesswork: first they had to return to the entrance hall to pick up the cases they'd forgotten. They looked a trifle sheepish as they did so. For some of their team-mates had jumped to the conclusion that Keith and Kevin had come back because they'd found something frightening upstairs.

Gary felt envious when he saw them together for he had hoped to share a room with Keith himself. He had to be content with Damian Cooke's company and perhaps that wasn't a bad thing, he consoled himself, for Damian was big enough to deal with any ghost that might visit them.

As captain, Crispin Jones chose to have a room on his own so that he could read as long as he wanted undisturbed and Lester Rowan hung back to the end so that he could have the same privilege—though for a different reason. If anyone shared with him Lester might be forced to reveal the secret of his box; and he was determined to avoid that as long as possible.

Damian led the way up a narrow, twisting staircase from the first floor in search of Room 13. Both he and Gary were thinking about that unlucky number and hoping that it didn't mean they were in for a terrible night. They spotted

Room 12 and, a little further along the corridor, Room 14. But Room 13 seemed to have vanished.

"There must be a Room 13, mustn't there?" Damian asked worriedly. He didn't like things to go wrong; his confidence in his ability to work out problems for himself didn't match his size.

Gary wasn't willing to give up yet. He crept along the passageway and turned a corner. The light was fairly dim at this point but he could just make out a narrow wooden staircase leading upwards. Beside it was a ladder which appeared to be propped against the side of a rectangular opening in the ceiling. Surely Room 13 couldn't be up *there*?

Reluctantly, Damian had followed him. They stood side by side and stared at the blackness of the hole and tried to imagine what lay beyond. It had to be an attic of some kind because they both sensed by now that they must be almost at the top of the building. Perhaps workmen had been carrying out some repairs on the roof.

"Let's try up there," Gary said bravely, stepping forward.

"What, up that ladder?" Damian asked in disbelief and horror.

"No, the staircase, you idiot," Gary replied. Now that he'd promoted himself to be the leader he was quite willing to go first. Anyway, he'd no intention of spending the night in a corridor. All the same, he took the stairs very slowly—with Damian breathing heavily right behind him.

The corridor at the top was very short and each of the three doors along it was clearly marked: Room 13; Bathroom; and Private.

"Great," said Gary, pushing open the first door, "we've found it! Hey, it's a real hideaway. Come and see."

The ceiling sloped sharply towards the far wall in which was set a single window, narrow enough to have been used once by bowmen defending the battlements.

On either side of the window was a narrow, single bed covered with a brightly-coloured bedspread, one in orange and the other in lemon. They helped to make up for the gloom of the rest of the room for the furniture was of dark, heavy oak and the wallpaper was a cheerless red. But to the boys it was an exciting place, not least because it seemed to be cut off from the rest of the hotel. It was almost like having a tiny house of their own.

When they'd changed into their pyjamas and visited the bathroom next door Damian sank down on to his bed and started to talk about the match with Bonchester. Normally, Gary was willing to talk football all night but now he was feeling very, very tired. Five minutes ago he'd felt quite energetic—he'd even done some press-ups in the bathroom—but suddenly he could hardly keep his eyes open.

"Look, I'm getting into bed," he told Damian. "Last one standing up turns the light off." And promptly he slid down between the sheets before Damian had a chance to beat him to it.

Damian had only wanted to talk because he felt a bit scared. The silence when neither of them was speaking was unnerving. At home, where he shared a room with two brothers, someone was always making a noise, even late at night.

But when Gary began to make some imitation snores to show that he really did want to go to sleep, Damian had no option but to switch off the light and hurriedly climb into his own bed. He should feel safe there.

He'd hardly closed his eyes when an owl hooted close by. In the surrounding silence it was a terrifying sound and Damian shrieked. He couldn't help it. He sat bolt upright and experienced a curious tingling feeling all over his body.

"What was that noise?" he gasped when at last he could speak. But there was no reply. Gary had his head under the bedclothes and hadn't heard the question. Damian was sure his friend must have died from the shock—either that or some mysterious, invisible ray had killed him.

Cautiously, he got out of bed and tip-toed across the gap to where Gary should be lying. Hands outstretched, he felt along the length of the bed, tracing Gary's shape. Still there was no movement. Then, when the owl hooted again— even more alarmingly this time—Damian jabbed desperately at what he guessed to be Gary's shoulder. In fact, it was his neck. Gary awoke with a flurry of arms and legs under the bedclothes. He thought someone was trying to murder him.

There was only just enough light in the room for him to be able to make out the sinister outline of someone bending over him. Now he was convinced that he was being attacked.

He was just about to yell for help—and fling himself out of the other side of the bed—when a terrible sound paralysed his vocal cords. It seemed to come from beyond his attacker—from somewhere on the far side of the room.

It was a high-pitched, wailing noise, rising and falling ... Weeeee-aaaahhhh-ayeayeayeaye-aaa-hhhh!

Damian collapsed across Gary's bed. Gary, realizing in that moment who his attacker was, clutched at him as though he was making a Rugby tackle. Together they stared across the dark room, fearful of what was going to happen next. Neither of them was now capable of moving a muscle to help themselves.

The awful noise died away—and was replaced by another just as horrifying. A gentle scrape, scr-ape, scra-pe, as if someone—or something—was trying to find a way into their room.

In his terror Damian suddenly found he could speak—although only in a whisper. In any case, he wouldn't have dared speak louder: the creature might have heard him and increased its efforts to get at him and Gary. Not that they had any doubt that it was determined to get to them. For the scraping was becoming quite frantic, as if it was now desperate to find a way in.

"It's a ghost—it must be—come to murder us to death," Damian whispered, no longer capable of choosing his words carefully.

"But ghosts aren't supposed to make a lot of noise," Gary replied, trying hard to keep a quaver out of his voice. "And why can't we see it? Ghosts are supposed to be dressed all in white and clank a chain or something round their leg."

As though coming in perfectly on cue, the creature (it had to be a creature because the boys couldn't believe it was human) made a rattling sound which might well have come from a chain.

"Oh, brother—it *is* a ghost!" Damian wailed, his voice now rising to an unexpected height.

The ghost responded to the recognition immediately.

Weeeeee-aaaahhhh-ayeayeayeaye-ooooOOOO!

Instinctively, Damian and Gary tried to scramble beneath the bed. It had occurred to neither of them to rush across the room and switch on the light. Because, by trying to cross the room, they'd have been within clutching distance of the ghost. They were no longer sure that it hadn't already entered their bedroom.

"What are we going to do when it starts to attack us?" asked Gary, preparing for the worst.

"Oh, don't ask me," Damian replied. "We'll just have to surrender and plead for mercy."

"Ghosts don't take prisoners," Gary said scathingly. He was rapidly coming to the conclusion that Damian was a bit of a softie—no, a complete softie. For all his size, he was going to be no help at all in the present situation.

Gary tried to work out a plan of escape. They couldn't get through the window—and, in any case, they were right at the top of the castle (he no longer thought of it as an hotel). So the only way out was through the door. Yet it was from that direction that the noises had been coming. All the same, he couldn't see any alternative to making a dash for it.

Suddenly, he realized that the ghost had been silent for quite some time. It hadn't made a single sound since that last awful wail. His hopes began to rise. Perhaps it had gone away—gone off to haunt someone else.

He was beginning to feel a bit foolish at cowering under the bed like a frightened cat. He nudged Damian in the ribs—and wasn't surprised to get a shriek of terror from his room-mate.

"I think it's gone," Gary said softly, still conscious of the fact that if it was still in the vicinity the ghost would hear what he was saying. "Let's get out of here while we can."

Damian didn't think much of that suggestion but, as he had no intention of remaining anywhere on his own, he crawled out from under the bed in Gary's wake.

They were just getting to their feet when they heard a strange scuffling sound somewhere beyond the door. Next moment the latch clicked —and the door began to swing open.

Five

The boys automatically clutched each other again. Once more they felt powerless to move as they stared, hypnotized, at the moving door and the faint light behind it.

They had no difficulty in seeing what was coming through the opening. For it was dressed all in white. From the top of the covered head to the invisible feet.

Dry-mouthed with terror, they shrank back—though their legs would hardly support them. And then the ghost utttered its appalling, inhuman sound.

Weeeee-aaaahhhhh-ayeayeayeaye-oooOOOO!

"Oh, spare us, please spare us," Damian pleaded. "We'll do anything you want—anything."

This time Gary was quite willing to be included in that appeal. His brain had been numbed but he knew that he was too young to die. His

79

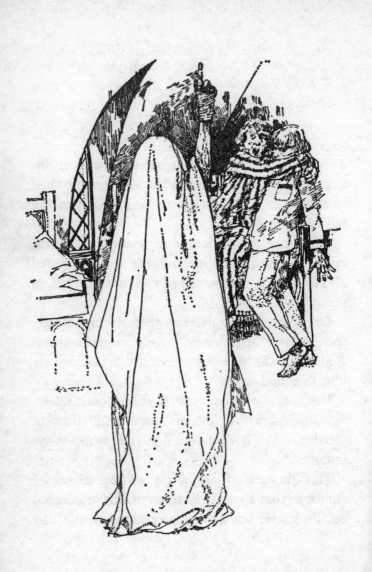

whole football career, his England cap, lay ahead of him.

The ghost had stopped moving. It appeared to be quivering. It would hardly be shaking from cold, Gary was now able to realize, because ghosts aren't supposed to feel changes in temperature. A split-second later he discovered that it had simply been preparing to speak.

"We are the Ghost of Grantley Castle," it announced in a surprisingly squeaky voice. "We have come to haunt you—to haunt you for ever and ever."

Damian suddenly found the courage, and the voice, to ask a question.

"But why? Why have you chosen us? What have we done wrong?"

The ghost did not reply immediately. It seemed to be considering what its answer should be.

Then: "You have offended us. That is why you must pay the penalty."

The last word was uttered almost as a shriek and Damian felt a chill that went right through to his bones. Gary, however, had remained quite remarkably calm during the last few moments. Now he decided it was time he asked a question.

"Where have you come from, Ghost of Grantley Castle—or whatever you call yourself?" he wanted to know. His voice was firm, his question direct.

The ghost hesitated a moment or two before answering this question, too. Then it flung up its right arm to point dramatically to the Heavens (or some secret abode above Room 13).

"Up there, where—" the ghost was proclaiming when, to Damian's utter amazement, Gary leapt at the white-covered figure—and knocked it to the ground.

"It's *you*, Kevin, you rat!" Gary was yelling excitedly. "I knew it was as soon as you said 'penalty'. You screamed it just like you do on the soccer pitch when you think you've been fouled in the box."

He was pummelling away at his Bank Vale United team-mate in his glee at discovering the ghost's identity. His fear had vanished the moment he'd heard that give-away word. Then, when Kevin had been foolish enough to move his arm to point upwards, Gary had also seen the bandage Kevin was still wearing. For that bandage was by no means as white as the sheet Kevin had covered himself with for the haunting expedition to Room 13.

Kevin tried to roll to one side to avoid the attack but he was hampered by the sheet which

82

had been wrapped round him very tightly. Nor was he able to defend himself and Gary's blows, though not delivered with full force, were beginning to hurt.

"Lay off, Gary," he yelled. "You're hurting my arm—the injured one. I won't be able to play in the next match, you idiot."

At that moment Keith Nash sneaked into the room: he was overjoyed that the haunting had worked so well but he didn't want the fighting to continue. Both combatants were now making a lot of noise and someone in the hotel would be sure to hear them.

He dived in to haul Gary out of the struggle. "Pack it in, now," he ordered. After all, he was the Bank Vale United captain and he was used to giving orders.

With a final cuff at Kevin's head, Gary stood up. But he made no effort to help Kevin to his feet. For his part, Damian had said nothing and done nothing. He seemed to be still getting over the shock of the arrival of the ghost, even though he knew now who that ghost was.

Kevin struggled to his feet, assisted by Keith, and then carefully wrapped the sheet round himself again. After the bout on the floor it was no longer very white. Kevin winced a couple of times as he tested his injured arm, and then grinned as he looked at Gary.

"It worked, didn't it?" he said triumphantly. "You were absolutely scared rotten. Didn't know what was happening, did you? It must be the best haunting there's ever been in this old castle!"

"Was it really you making that funny noise through there?" Damian asked, pointing to the far wall. He hadn't quite got over his worst fears.

" 'Course it was," Kevin told him, with much satisfaction in his voice. "It was great that the ladder was there. It leads up to a sort of opening just under the roof—and right next door to this room. We knew you were up here because we came to check first."

"Was that you hooting like an owl then?" Damian persisted.

" 'Course it was—" Kevin was beginning to boast again when Keith, with his usual direct honesty, admitted that the hooting owl had been a bit of luck for them. "Actually, it, er—er, it surprised us a bit, as well," he confessed. That was as near as he was going to get to acknowledging that he and Kevin had been scared, too.

"Right," said Kevin, eager as ever to keep

things moving, "who shall we go and haunt next? This place is riddled with ladders and trap doors —it's perplexing how nobody's disappeared yet. There's bound to be some secret passages as well. If we can find one of them we could get right into someone else's room without going through the door. That's the proper way for a ghost to arrive."

They were just starting to think about that, and who might be the best victim, when, from not so far away, they heard a curious sound.

A soft, but perfectly audible, shhlip, shhhlip, shhlip. It was accompanied by another noise. SSShh-uh, sssshhh-uh, ssssshhhhh-uh.

Now, none of them dare speak. They glanced at each other in the pale light from beyond the door and the fear had returned to the eyes of Gary and Damian—and arrived on the faces of Kevin and Keith. All of them were thinking much the same thing.

A real ghost was coming to haunt them!

Sssshhh-uh ... ssslip ... sshhhlip.

It was getting nearer.

Instinctively, Damian and Gary moved back to be nearer their beds. They had hidden under them once and they were ready to do so again.

Although the light was not strong enough to reveal it, Kevin's face had gone whiter than the sheet he was still wearing. Keith, too, moved away from the door and edged towards his friends. He knew now what was meant by the phrase "safety in numbers". Being with others at a time like this was much better than being on your own. He'd worked out that the ghost could hardly attack all four of them at once. But if he remained nearest the door he would be the first victim.

Sssssshhh-uh ... sssshhh-lip ... ssshhhlip.

It was coming up the stairs and it was almost at the top.

Together, the boys herded to the back of the room, as close as possible to the narrow window.

None of them had thought to close the door. But even if they had, they'd have remembered that a closed door is no barrier to a determined ghost. A real ghost can pass through stone walls when it wants to.

"Oh, I wish we'd never come here," Damian began to moan softly. "I wish I was safe at home in my own bed. We never get ghosts at our house."

"It might be scared when it sees me all in white," Kevin muttered, hopefully. But he didn't really believe that would happen. The real ghost might pick on him first for doing impersonations.

Suddenly, the strange noises stopped—and they began to think the ghost had changed its mind about visiting them.

But the ghost was only getting its breath back after the effort of climbing all those steep steps. It was pausing before entering the boys' room. But it wasn't dressed all in white: it was wearing all-black.

For the four boys anxiously awaiting their first glimpse, the identity of their visitor was just as great a shock as if it had been the most fearsome ghost in the world.

"I thought as much," puffed Miss O'Houlihan as she stood in the doorway and surveyed them. "I just knew it. I knew I couldn't trust a bunch of football hooligans in my hotel."

Not for the first time that night the boys were struck dumb. If a vote had been taken at that moment it would have shown that they'd have preferred a ghost to Miss O'Houlihan.

She looked at them coldly through her clip-on spectacles and her gaze came to rest on Kevin. He'd expected that. His mother would have reacted in exactly the same way if she'd found him garbed in one of her bed sheets. One of her *best* bed sheets, of course: she'd have insisted that he'd deliberately made things worse by choosing the best for his "capers" (one of her favourite words).

"You, boy!" Miss O'Houlihan shot at him. "What do you mean by covering yourself in one of my best bed sheets and getting it filthy with your disgusting games?"

Kevin sighed. He would have shrugged as well but in the half-light and under the cover of the sheet a shrug wouldn't have been noticed. Anyway, Miss O'Houlihan was not the sort of person who would accept a gesture for an answer.

"Sorry, Miss," he mumbled.

"*Sorry*," she snorted. "Is that all you can say? And I suppose you were also the one who was making that positively disgusting noise that we heard all over the hotel. Shrieking like a Zulu warrior."

Nobody said anything. After all, it hadn't exactly been a question.

"Well," Miss O'Houlihan insisted, "aren't you going to have the decency to own up to your crimes?"

"I'm sorry, Miss," Kevin mumbled again. He just wished that somebody else would admit to something. It wasn't fair that he should be accused of everything. He'd managed to forget that he'd arranged most of the ghostly haunting.

"I think you should remember that I have a name," she said stiffly. "I'm not just 'Miss', like one of your school mistresses. I'm Miss O'Houlihan. And I like to be addressed by my name, boy."

Kevin bit his lip and grimaced at the same time. It really was rotten the way she was just picking on him. But he knew he'd be in deeper trouble if she were to tell Mr Gregsten that, in addition to his other crimes, he'd been cheeky to her.

"Sorry, Miss Ghouligan," he said, as clearly as he could.

Her gasp coincided with Keith Nash's explosive giggle. Keith hadn't meant to giggle: he simply couldn't help it. He and Kevin had decided earlier between themselves that Miss O'Houlihan was a bit ghoulish. It was a slip of the tongue by Kevin to call her Miss Ghouligan—but it really fitted her perfectly.

It was Keith she turned on now. "So you think that sheer insolence is funny, do you, boy?" she thundered at him. "Well, we'll see what your teacher has to say about that. What is your name, young man?"

"Er—Keith Nash, Miss. I mean, Miss O'Houlihan."

"Right, Master Nash. I shall remember that

name. And you—" turning back to Kevin—
"what's your name?"

Kevin told her—and this time managed to pro-
nounce her name correctly. He didn't blame
Keith for laughing. It was a great story to tell
the other lads in the morning, whatever fate was
in store for him for offending her.

"Right," she repeated. "Now, you can get off
to your own rooms this instant. We've all spent
long enough out of our beds because of your
wicked tricks. And if I hear another sound—just
one more noise—from any of you before breakfast time in the morning then you'll wish you'd
never been born, believe me. Now, get off with
you—and take that sheet off, Ripley."

They departed at top speed as soon as Kevin
had divested himself of his ghost's haunting gear.
All the time Miss O'Houlihan had been interro-
gating their friends, Gary and Damian had been
wondering what was going to happen to themselves. Although they were innocent of causing
any trouble they couldn't be sure that Miss
O'Houlihan would be fair-minded enough to
realize that. But she could find only a minor fault
with them.

"Right, you two," she said crisply, "get back
into your own beds. And don't open that door

again to anyone this night. We've had enough stupidity tonight to last us a lifetime."

"Yes, Miss O'Houlihan," they responded dutifully, and hurried to obey her. She was good enough to wish them goodnight as she closed the door behind her. They made no attempt to chat about what had happened. And within minutes they were fast asleep.

For the rest of the night, guests and staff at the Grantley Hotel slept undisturbed. When the owl hooted again no one was awake to hear it.

At breakfast time the first boys to reach the dining-room had plenty to talk about. But by now the stories of Miss O'Houlihan's temper and her late-night round-up had made such an impression on them that they talked only in whispers.

No one dared laugh aloud when Kevin recounted, for the umpteenth time, his tale of addressing her as "Miss Ghouligan". All the same, he won all the admiration he'd been seeking. Until, that is, Mr Gregsten walked in. Miss O'Houlihan had already spoken to him in private so he was fully informed on the subject of the night's outrages. He had asked for, and been given, the names of the chief offenders.

He called for, and got, immediate and complete attention. He then delivered the sort of lecture that a First Division Manager might justifiably have given to his team after they'd been knocked out of the Cup by a bunch of part-timers. "You miserable lot" was one of his favourite expressions and he gave full rein to it. By half-time they were all convinced that the tour was over and they were being sent home immediately. For Keith Nash, the worst was yet to come.

"As for you, Nash," Mr Gregsten said, "I can only say I'm astonished at your lack of responsibility. I made you vice-captain because I thought you were sensible and capable of showing powers of leadership. An error on my part, obviously.

"You showed as much commonsense as my dog chasing a cat across a motorway. In other words, you played the idiot, whether it was you or Ripley who had the idea of acting the goat—ghost, I mean."

Because none of them could be certain that Mr Gregsten's slip was intended to be a joke nobody laughed. After all, he still looked fierce.

"So, Nash," he went on, "I'm taking the vice-captaincy away from you, not only to punish you but as an example to every boy on this tour that I won't stand for any nonsense that upsets people—people like Miss O'Houlihan, who was doing her best to make us all comfortable in this hotel.

"I'm telling you all now—and I mean every word of it—that if there's any repetition of the sort of thing that happened last night at any of the other places we're staying at, then the tour will be over for everyone. We shall go straight home—and your parents will be told *why* we've returned early."

That was the moment that Crispin Jones chose to stroll in; he was the last to arrive for breakfast, but perhaps he considered that was a captain's privilege.

Mr Gregsten, his anger not entirely evaporated, glanced at him and asked if he'd slept well.

"Oh yes," Crispin replied. "It was a bit before I dropped off. I started to read a ghost book. It was jolly good to start with—but then—well—" Amazingly, Crispin for once seemed lost for words.

"You mean you didn't finish it?" Mr Gregsten asked, as surprised as everyone else by this curious attitude of Crispin's.

"Er, no, I didn't, actually," Crispin admitted. "Funny, really, but this place seemed creepy enough without reading about other people's ghosts. So I started reading a book of jokes instead and laughed myself to sleep."

For a moment, every breath was held. And then Mr Gregsten laughed.

After that, the usual chatter broke out among the boys. But when breakfast was served none of them felt able to complain that one scrap of bacon, some tinned tomatoes and one piece of toast was hardly enough for hungry young footballers.

Miss O'Houlihan had had the last word in her own way.

Six

Keith Nash was feeling better—but not much better. In the thirty hours that had passed since he'd lost the vice-captaincy of the Town Boys' team he'd felt more miserable than at any time in his life. He was convinced that he wouldn't be picked for either of the two matches that remained to be played on the tour. But Mr Gregsten had just announced the team for the game against Crowley—and Keith was among the players selected.

So, rather to his own surprise, was Kevin Ripley. He, too, had expected to be punished for his part in the Grantley Hotel haunting escapade but, after being given a severe personal lecture by the team manager, he was told he was to play at centre-forward in place of Robert Tranfield. Kevin made a private vow that he would score at least three goals before half-time.

Gary Ansell had also been dropped, or "rested",

as Mr Gregsten described it, and replaced by Peter Starbrook. Gary was furious. He thought he had been treated unfairly—doubly unfairly, as he muttered to himself. For he was out of the team after causing no trouble at all at the hotel, while the real trouble-makers, Kevin and Keith, were both playing. What's more, his position had been given to a player, Peter Starbrook, who normally played not as a winger but as a striker. To Gary it was no consolation at all to be told by Mr Gregsten that he was to be substitute and might be called on later in the game.

There were two other changes from the side that had beaten Bonchester so convincingly. Andrew Margain was in goal and at right-back Mark Maskell had taken over from Gavin Streeter.

When the teams took the field on another warm afternoon Mr Gregsten formed the opinion that several of the Crowley boys were a good deal older than his own players. Some of them were almost as tall as himself and he was thankful he had included such a powerful boy as Peter Starbrook in his forward line—and he rather wished he'd kept Tranfield at centre-forward instead of bringing in the fairly slightly-built Kevin Ripley. But he knew that Kevin would play his heart out and give as good as he got if any knocks were being handed out.

Crowley, who'd obviously heard about the game at Bonchester and so knew that Town Boys had conceded an early goal, were determined to make a good start and assert their superiority. Damian Cooke, who just might still have been suffering from the effects of his bad scare during the night, was bundled off the ball in the opening seconds. Town Boys should have been awarded a free kick for the offence but the referee took no action. He believed that schoolboys should always play the game vigorously and not moan about unimportant fouls.

When Keith Nash was felled from behind by another furious tackle and, again, the referee did nothing about it, Mr Gregsten began to get worried about what sort of game this was going to be. Nash had certainly dithered when he should have got clear with the ball but that didn't excuse the foul that Crowley committed against him.

In the first ten minutes all the attacking was done by Crowley and their supporters, who'd turned up in good numbers, were yelling continuously for a goal. After their early stumbles Nash and Cooke recovered to play quite soundly but the best defensive work was coming from Mark Maskell, the new full-back (or sweeper, as he liked to describe himself). Twice he prevented almost certain goals by first heading off the line and then making a desperate tackle in the box without using the sort of tactics that Crowley seemed to favour.

Mr Gregsten's worry now was the form of Andrew Margain in goal. The boy had not been his personal choice to make the tour as No. 2 goalkeeper for in Mr Gregsten's opinion Margain lacked courage, a quality that no goalkeeper could afford to be without. He was also inclined to shout too many orders to his co-defenders. "Let me see 'em coming," was his favourite call. Mr Gregsten guessed that the boy had picked the phrase up while watching second-rate players who thought they were imitating First Division footballers.

Now, as the ball was lofted into the penalty area yet again, Margain stayed on his line when he should have come out either to catch the ball or punch it clear. Only another fine clearance by Maskell saved the situation. By now Kevin Ripley, hungry for the ball, had dropped back into mid-field in the hope of picking up a pass there. So far the Town forwards hadn't had a chance of showing what they could do. And Kevin wasn't going to wait for ever.

His foraging paid off eventually. In a tussle with his opposite number in the Crowley team Kevin refused to give in and when he came away with the ball he accelerated up-field. This was his first opportunity on the tour to show what he could do and he was going to make the most of it.

The sight of Kevin heading for goal (even though he still had a long way to go) inspired his team-mates. At last they could move out of their own half—and most of them did so. But no sooner had they crossed the halfway line than Kevin lost the ball as two Crowley defenders closed in on him. The player who actually gained possession wasted not a moment in turning defence into attack. He booted the ball back into the Town Boys' half of the field where it was picked up cleverly by the Crowley centre-forward. He swerved past Damian Cooke with alarming ease and went in a straight line for the penalty area.

Mark Maskell was the only defender who'd stayed well back, although some of his colleagues were now returning as fast as they could run. But they had no chance of overtaking the fleet-footed centre-forward who delighted in making solo runs. Andrew Margain was dancing up and down on his line as he watched the Crowley player advance on him. As Mark began to move forward Andrew pleaded with him to stay where he was. Mark hesitated—fatally. For, as he tried to make up his mind how and when to tackle, the Crowley centre-forward nipped round him. Now only Andrew stood between him and his objective —the back of the net.

Andrew, too, should have come out to narrow the angle for the shot but his hesitation was as bad as the sweeper's. The centre-forward was picking his spot for his shot when, at last, Andrew hurled himself forward.

His attempt at a save looked both brave and spectacular—and it actually succeeded for the ball didn't go into the net. It bounced harmlessly off his shoulder for a corner. But the Crowley player's kicking foot buried itself in Andrew's upper arm.

The goalkeeper yelped with pain as he collapsed on the ground and began writhing in agony. Mr Gregsten, showing an unexpected burst of speed across the pitch, was the second person to reach the injured player. Crowley's centre-forward himself was already doing all he could to apologize and comfort the stricken goalie. He knew it was an accident, and not his fault at all, but he didn't like hurting anyone.

Mr Gregsten carried out some quick checks and was satisfied that no bones were broken. But he didn't doubt that Andrew really was in a great deal of pain. It had been a strong kick. He helped Andrew off the pitch and asked someone to fetch a pain-killing spray. When the referee came up Mr Gregsten said that he would want to bring on his reserve goalkeeper. The referee nodded; the substitution of a goalkeeper was permitted at any time in these friendly matches.

But, as he glanced round, the Town Boys' Manager could see no sign of Lester Rowan, who should have been somewhere among the spectators. Since the match started Mr Gregsten had been too absorbed in the play to take note of what his four reserve players were doing.

He had no idea that Lester had been absent since a few minutes after the kick-off.

"Where's Lester Rowan?" he demanded to know.

"He's gone off somewhere, sir," Robert Tranfield told him quite eagerly.

Mr Gregsten could hardly believe it. "Gone *off* somewhere? He can't have, there's nowhere to go round here. Has he gone to the toilet?"

"No, sir," Robert assured him. "I saw Rowan going off to the bus-stop. He wouldn't say where he was going but he was catching a bus."

It was, as Kevin might have said, perplexing. But Mr Gregsten had no time to waste looking for a missing boy; the matter would have to be dealt with later. What he had to decide now was who was going to take over in goal. It would have to be a forward—and his choice fell on Nick Abel-Smith. Nick could jump and he could handle a ball.

Nick wasn't pleased at being removed from the forward line. His job was to score goals, not save them. He had a poor opinion of defenders and he felt it was an insult to be turned into one. But Mr Gregsten was in no mood for an argument. He ordered Nick to put the green jersey on and take up his position between the posts.

In sharp contrast to Nick's gloom, Gary Ansell was overjoyed. For he was called on as substitute to take Nick's place in the forward line. With Starbrook on the wing, Gary would now operate as a strike-forward in the middle alongside Kevin. That suited him perfectly. If he managed to score a couple of goals he would keep his place for the next match.

Nick's first job was to deal with the corner

kick that had resulted from Andrew's dive. He took little note of where his co-defenders were stationing themselves and he momentarily relaxed when he saw that Crowley were taking a short corner with the winger pushing the ball back to a team-mate. But the centre that came in from that player was a good one. As the ball dropped, Nick and Crowley's centre-forward jumped for it together. They collided in mid-air without either of them making contact with it.

They both fell, with the Crowley player landing heavily on top of his opponent. It looked like another accident but there was a suspicion in the minds of some of the onlookers that the centre-forward had fallen that way deliberately. While the ball was being scrambled away, he made his usual offer of help to an opponent he'd knocked about a bit but Nick pushed him away angrily. The new goalkeeper was winded and suffering from a pain in his thigh but he wasn't going to complain about it. That wasn't his way. As long as he could move about he would stay in the game. All the same, he wouldn't forget who'd caused the pain.

During the course of the next few attacks by the Crowley forwards Nick was relieved to see that the defence had tightened up considerably.

While attending to Andrew, Mr Gregsten had given instructions that defenders were to stay back and not give their opponents chances to build an attack.

His words had sunk in for players like Keith Nash, Graham Connally and Jonathan Castree were now tackling like demons. Adrian Dawnay had dropped back to reinforce the middle line and the Crowley forwards were being kept at bay.

Crowley's centre-forward, who seemed to have boundless energy, was constantly switching from wing to wing, searching for a loop-hole. His place in the middle had been taken by the inside-right, who didn't appear to possess anything like the centre-forward's speed. Damian wasn't certain whether he should continue to shadow the centre-forward or concentrate now on the inside-right. He'd been told many times in tactical talks that his job was to guard the middle. But Damian had seen for himself that the roving centre-forward was the greatest danger to Town Boys.

Suddenly, however, it was the Crowley left-winger who was cutting through. When Keith went to tackle him the winger exchanged passes very smartly with his inside-forward partner and then kept to his line as he moved deeper into the Town Boys' territory.

Crowley's centre-forward, anticipating a pass soon, swerved away from the left flank and raced to the edge of the box. The inside-right was merely lumbering up the middle and, in Damian's eyes, was no threat at all. The centre-forward was the one who had to be watched—and checked as soon as the ball was sent to him. And when Damian moved to his right Mark Maskell was slow to come across to cover the centre.

The winger slowed fractionally, looked up—and then hit the ball fiercely across the penalty area.

It was clearly intended for the centre-forward, who could shoot effectively with either foot, and Damian was congratulating himself on his powers of anticipation, for he was almost alongside Crowley's inside-right as the ball reached the centre-forward. But he fooled Damian, and almost everyone else, by simply jumping over the ball and allowing it to run across the box.

The one player who hadn't been fooled was the inside-right. This was a trick he and Crowley's centre-forward had worked successfully in other matches. For the inside-right could do a fast sprint when it was necessary. Now he darted forward, took the ball in his stride and positively hammered it into the net past the helpless goalkeeper.

Nick couldn't be blamed for the goal in any way for the shot would have beaten most experienced 'keepers—and no other defender had been anywhere near the Crowley player.

Nick picked the ball out of the net and savagely punted it back to the centre. The Crowley players were surging round the inside-right and the centre-forward with their congratulations while

Damian Cooke and Mark Maskell were hoping that Mr Gregsten hadn't noticed their mistakes.

But Mr Gregsten missed very little and at half-time, with Crowley still leading 1-0, he told Damian that for the rest of the game he was to stick as close to the centre-forward as a stamp to an envelope. He'd also spotted some other weaknesses in his team—Keith was to stop wandering out to the wing; Jonathan Castree was to use the long pass out of defence as soon as he got clear with the ball—and he was making sure that all the players knew what was expected of them in the second half.

Yet none of his advice was of any help to them five minutes after the resumption. Crowley had started slowly, allowing Town Boys to make the running, and then they struck again from inside their own half. Their centre-half was exceptionally strong and the free kick he took sent the ball well down the field. The left-winger came in to hook it first time into the penalty area where the centre-forward rose above Damian. Once again, though, he made no attempt to score himself. He nodded the ball across the face of the goal—and the inside-right, who'd been stealing in from the right, leapt forward to flick it neatly with his head beyond Nick's reach.

This time Nick complained bitterly about the lack of cover from his defenders. His remarks were so cutting that Jonathan Castree, normally one of the mildest players in the team, told him to shut up. "You're not the Manager—or the captain," he pointed out.

"And you're useless in defence," Nick retaliated, eyes flashing. He was still in pain but that mattered less to him than the fact that his team were two-down. Nick Abel-Smith hated to lose.

By now the heart had gone out of some of the Town players and Mr Gregsten, recognizing the symptoms, knew that this was one match his team wasn't going to win. There was nothing he could tell them now that would put them back in the game. Yet there was still some satisfaction to be gained from the match. For the forwards began to work harder than ever to pull one goal back.

Crispin Jones, who'd been having a very easy time so far, suddenly started appearing everywhere. It was when he turned up on the right wing, having detected a weakness in Crowley's left-back, that Mr Gregsten was able to smile for the first time since the match began.

Twice Crispin pushed the ball towards the full-back—and the back stretched for it eagerly. But Crispin was only tormenting him for each time he rolled the ball back with the sole of his boot. He swerved to go left, he swerved to go to the right, and finally spun round in a complete circle, leaving the dazed full-back lying flat out on the turf. Other Crowley defenders had closed in now—if rather warily—but Crispin had no intention of keeping possession any longer.

He slammed the ball right across the penalty area. Gary Ansell, diving full-length quite spectacularly, deflected the ball with his head, right into the path of Kevin. And Kevin crashed it into the roof of the net from close range. The two forwards congratulated each other ecstatically, forgetting for the moment that it was Crispin who had made the goal.

But they were right to make the most of it for it was the only goal Town Boys scored in the match, although they were pressing strongly for the equalizer when the final whistle blew.

Until he saw Nick Abel-Smith limping across the pitch Mr Gregsten had been thinking only about his team's defeat. Then he remembered his missing player.

"Where on earth has Lester Rowan got to?" he wanted to know.

Seven

Long before the bus reached the town centre, Lester Rowan was looking anxiously at his watch. The organizers had told him in their letter that Perkins would have to be taken before the judges no later than 2.30 p.m. It was now well past two o'clock and Lester wasn't even in Crowley yet. He wished, for the umpteenth time, that the showground had been closer to the football ground.

Perkins was a guinea pig. He was the best guinea pig that Lester had owned. He was a champion. At the moment he was resting in his special wooden carrying-box on the seat beside Lester. He was contentedly bedded down on straw, nibbling a fresh young carrot from the supply that Lester had bought with his pocket-money that morning. And if Perkins should wish for a change of diet there was lettuce and dandelion leaves in a polythene bag in Lester's pocket. Perkins always had to have the best of everything.

Before breakfast that morning Lester had spent almost half-an-hour grooming his favourite guinea pig—combing and brushing the beautiful black-and-brown-and-white fur of the animal. Perkins was an Abyssinian and far handsomer, in Lester's opinion, than the popular smooth-haired

guinea pigs owned by some of his friends (and rivals, as he thought of them). Perkins would also have been given a wet shampoo if there'd been time—and no fear of interruption from any of his Town Boys' team-mates.

It had been difficult enough to keep Perkins' presence a secret from the other players. Robert Tranfield especially had been a persistent pest. Lester was grateful to Mr Livingstone, the coach-driver, who had looked after Perkins during the game against Bonchester. He had been very helpful on other occasions, too, for it turned out that his own daughters also kept guinea pigs and he himself quite liked "these neat little creatures", as he described them.

In fact, Lester decided, things had really worked out very well indeed. For he had calculated that he wouldn't be needed for the second match of the tour and therefore he would be free to enter Perkins at Crowley Show, which was being held at the same time as the soccer match.

Accordingly, he had written off the previous week to the organizers of the Cavy Section (guinea pigs were known as cavies) and asked for an entry form. The organizers were quite impressed to receive an entry from so far away—though not nearly so impressed as Lester's friends would be if Perkins won a prize at a Show in another county. They entered their pets only in local shows but Lester was much more ambitious.

It was because Lester had shown such enterprise that the organizers had agreed to allow him to bring Perkins to the Show after the normal closing time for entries. But they had stipulated that 2.30 p.m. had to be the absolute deadline.

Lester checked his watch again : 2.20. But now they were turning into the bus station. With

Perkins tucked up in his box under his arm, Lester was down on the platfrom, ready to jump off the bus as soon as it pulled into its bay. Luckily, an inspector was waiting there and Lester asked him where he could catch a bus for the Showground.

"Just over there, son," the inspector said, pointing to an adjacent bay. "But hurry—the bus is just about to leave."

Lester caught it as it was moving off and was thankful that the journey took only five minutes. When he reached the main entrance, and showed his exhibitor's pass, it was 2.28. To his dismay, however, the Cavy Section was located on the far side of the arena. He had never run so fast in his life and people who jumped out of his way imagined that something terrible must have happened to him to make him run like that. For Lester, nothing could be more terrible than missing the deadline after all the trouble he'd taken to enter Perkins in Crowley Show.

It was 2.30 precisely when he dashed into the marquee and skidded to a halt in front of the judges' table. For a moment he couldn't speak, he was so out of breath, but the senior judge guessed who he was.

He smiled warmly and held out his hand for

the guinea pig. "You must be Master Rowan with an Abyssinian called Perkins, I imagine," he said. "Well, young man, we shall be most interested to meet him. We certainly admire your timing. We'd just about given you up!"

While the judges got on with their judging Lester wandered round the marquee. There were rows and rows of cages containing all manner

of guinea pigs and rabbits and mice. He stopped for a long time in front of a box containing a massive creature—an enormously long-eared Belgian hare that was much bigger than many full-grown cats. But his attention was really concentrated on the guineas.

From his experience of many other Shows, he could tell that Perkins had a lot of competition. There were many guinea pigs here that he would love to own. All the same, he believed that Perkins had a chance of picking up something. After all, he had won prizes before and, on one glorious occasion at a local event, had received the prize for Best Juvenile in the Show. He had also collected a first prize and a third prize and three highly commendeds. What worried Lester was the effect all the rushing this afternoon might have had on Perkins. He wasn't used to being carried at high speed in a small box. Nor, come to that, was he used to travelling on a motor-coach and living in hotel bedrooms.

Still, Perkins had looked well enough when Lester handed him over to the judge: his nose was twitching as rapidly as ever and his eyes were as bright as jewels.

It would be an hour or so before the results were announced and Lester decided to find a lemonade stall—and then have a look at the cat and dog sections. He rather liked cats and thought he might save up and buy one to enter in shows.

When he returned to the Cavy Section he walked very slowly, not at all certain of what the judges would have decided about Perkins. It would be rather dreadful to come all this way with his favourite guinea pig and then be told that he wasn't good enough to be placed in the first four.

But Lester needn't have worried. The judge saw him come in and immediately said: "Well done,

Lester. Your Perkins is a very fine specimen. You obviously know how to look after him. So we've given him first prize."

Lester was thrilled. It was the best result he'd ever had because he had seen the quality of Perkins' rivals. Now, he really had something to show his friends at home: a First Prize at Crowley Show! He also received a voucher for 50p but that was unimportant as far as he was concerned —though the money would be useful for buying more equipment for his hobby.

As he fondled Perkins before putting him back in his carrying-box he came to the conclusion that all the travelling must have done him some good for there was no doubt that Perkins looked in fine condition. He headed happily for the bus station with his first prizewinner and wondered whether Town Boys had won their match. It was the first time since lunch that he'd thought about football.

Eight

"If we lose this match today it'll mean that we shall return from our tour with more defeats than wins," Mr Gregsten pointed out. "And nobody at home is going to be very pleased about that. Quite a lot of people will think we've been wasting our time, or that we've got a very poor team. So I'm relying on you to beat Rainhurst this afternoon. Two victories in three matches is not a bad record."

Every member of the Town Boys' tour party listened to him with the utmost attention. Since their defeat, two days ago, by Crowley, their Manager had been in a bad mood. He'd told them all that there was only one thing he hated more than losing—and that was being let down by someone he trusted. In his opinion, Lester Rowan had let everyone down by disappearing when he'd been needed. With an experienced goal-keeper to replace the injured Andrew Margain, the team could have beaten Crowley, he said.

The fact that Lester had returned with a first prize from Crowley Show hadn't impressed Mr Gregsten at all (though some of the boys—including, surprisingly, Robert Tranfield—had been full of admiration for Perkins and his feat in winning an award). Indeed, since then Lester had been bombarded with inquiries about guinea pigs: where to buy them, what to feed them on and how to prepare them to win prizes. Naturally, the idea of picking up prize money was very appealing as a means of supplementing pocket-money.

Now, however, Lester dare not think about anything else but football. He was in the side for the game with Rainhurst because Andrew had not recovered from his injury and still had his arm in a sling.

The team showed one or two changes from the previous match. Nick Abel-Smith, too, was on the injured list. Although he had tried to shrug off his thigh injury he was still feeling pain when he moved and it had been aggravated by another knock received during a brief seven-a-side practice session earlier in the day. On that occasion, he had again been keeping goal because, Mr Gregsten had explained, there wasn't anyone who could do the job better. In truth, the Manager wanted to make sure he had a capable substitute on hand in case anything happened to Lester Rowan.

Jonathan Castree had been dropped, with Gavin Streeter taking his place in the middle-line. Robert Tranfield was back at centre-forward but Gary Ansell, to his enormous relief, had merely been switched back to his place on the right-wing with Peter Starbrook reverting to the role of substitute. Kevin, of course, was still thinking about scoring goals. It had never occurred to him that his own selection could have been in any doubt.

Although they would insist at home that they'd enjoyed every minute of the tour, and they wished it could have gone on for ever, some of the boys were beginning to feel just a little bit weary. They had discovered that it could be quite tiring to keep changing from one hotel to another; to make long journeys in a motor-coach; and to play three important matches in five days on top of practice sessions.

One or two were even feeling rather homesick, though they'd never have admitted that to anyone.

Everyone wanted to round off the tour with a great win. They wanted it for the Manager as well as for themselves. All things considered, they decided that Mr Gregsten had acted pretty reasonably during the tour. He'd been angry once or twice (particularly after that first night at Bonchester) but perhaps that anger had been justified. He'd been generous in letting them go off on their own for an hour or so each day and he'd even lent one or two of them some of his own money when they'd overspent. What he didn't know yet was that they'd all had a whip-round to buy him a present as a souvenir of the tour.

They'd bought a leather wallet and were going to present it to him just before they reached home. For Mr Livingstone, the coach-driver, they'd bought a map as a joke; but when Crispin had handed that over, and they'd all had a good laugh, they were going to give him his real present—a tie in orange-and-blue, the team's colours, which they'd found that morning in a shop in Rainhurst.

"Right," said Mr Gregsten, concluding his pre-match pep talk in the dressing-room, "it's up to you now. I want you to go out there and give everything you've got. After this match you'll have the chance of a long holiday from football, so you can use up all the energy you possess. We don't know just how good Rainhurst are but if you all play as well as you did against Bonchester then you ought to win."

For the first time since the tour began the sun had stopped shining and, as the teams ran out on to the pitch, the first spots of rain were falling. Lester Rowan turned and dashed back towards the dressing-room to the amazement of all his team-mates as well as Mr Gregsten.

"He must have forgotten to say goodbye to Perkins," remarked Robert Tranfield, unsure whether he was making a joke or speaking the truth.

When Lester returned a few moments later Mr Gregsten called to him. "Rowan, you haven't been attending to that rodent of yours again, have you?"

Lester shook his head violently. "Oh no, sir. I went back to fetch my gloves. I might need them if the ball's greasy."

"Oh, er, yes," Mr Gregsten agreed. "Good thinking, goalie."

The first goalkeeper to handle the ball in the match, however, was Rainhurst's. From the kick-off Town Boys went straight on to the attack, with Kevin switching the ball to the left-wing for Crispin to move in and pick it up. Crispin had been thinking that it was about time he scored a goal himself, although usually he was content to set up the chances for others to take.

His dribbling skill was always worth watching —unless you were one of his opponents. The Rainhurst defenders surged towards him but Crispin was rarely worried by numbers. The individual strength and timing of a tackle was what mattered. He beat two opponents by his body-swerve and ball control before the third, in desperation, almost knocked him to the ground in an effort to win the ball.

The referee, who had no intention of allowing any rough play to mar the match, blew for a foul—and that suited Crispin very well. He took the kick himself and lifted the ball to the back of the penalty area.

Robert Tranfield, who'd been warned what to expect, jumped to head the ball down to Kevin Ripley. Most times, Kevin would simply have hit the ball on the half-volley, blasting it towards the net for all he was worth. But one thing he had learned on this tour was not to be selfish. So this time he used his left foot to switch the ball back to the right for Gary Ansell to try a shot. It was good thinking for Gary was better placed than Kevin—and his well-struck shot would have gone into the net but for a superlative save by the Rainhurst goalie who palmed it round the far post at full stretch.

It was an exhilarating opening to the match and Mr Gregsten joined warmly in the applause. Gary, thrilled at having come so close to scoring with his first touch of the ball, took particular care with his corner kick. The ball dropped just short of the near-post. Kevin nipped across to try and head it on, but the right-back reached it ahead of him and hooked the ball clear. It went only as far as Keith Nash, on the edge of the box, and he immediately drove it back into the middle. Robert and Kevin and the Rainhurst centre-half clashed in the scramble to gain possession and for several anxious moments the ball bobbed about in the danger zone.

There was nothing scientific about the football being played at this stage: it was all kick-and-rush, push-and-scramble. Inevitably, someone was going to commit a foul—and that someone turned out to be Kevin. In his eagerness to stab the ball into the net his foot caught the goalkeeper's knee —and it was the referee's whistle that stemmed all the protests and accusations.

As the goalie was still hopping around from the effects of his injury, the kick was taken by a full-back. But it wasn't a good one. The ball went only as far as Damian Cooke, who'd come up in support of his forwards during the assault on the Rainhurst goal. Damian steadied himself, and then hit a long pass to Gary on the right. Gary pounced on it eagerly and went arrow-straight for the dead-ball line. When a defender came to head him off Gary swerved round him and then, without slowing down, swept the ball into the centre.

It reached Robert at waist-height and although he jumped he couldn't connect properly. The ball bounced off his knee and shot away to the left. Crispin, who'd been coming in from his wing, saw that the ball was now going to pass behind him. He spun instantly in a half-circle—and fell backwards as he just managed to hook his left foot under the ball. All he'd been trying to do was to keep the ball in play or, at best, send it back towards Robert. He achieved more than that.

For the ball passed over his head as it described a perfect arc in dropping just under the crossbar and into the furthest corner of the net.

Crispin had to admit to himself (though to no one else) that it was a lucky goal. Once before in his career he'd scored with a scissors kick, but

that had been intentional. His team-mates, of course, regarded it as a marvellous goal—and so, for that matter, did Mr Gregsten.

As far as Crispin was concerned, that goal merely whetted his appetite for more. He was aware that it had considerably deflated Rainhurst and they would be vulnerable to another attack if it came quickly. As soon as Keith Nash won the ball in midfield Crispin called for it. Defenders immediately converged on him but Crispin instantly laid the ball off to Kevin, received a return pass, beat another man by pushing the ball past him and then running the other way, before finally sending Kevin clear with a perfectly-judged through ball.

It was the chance Kevin had dreamed about and he wasn't going to waste it. He raced into the penalty area, dummied his way round the centre-half (the only opponent, apart from the goal-keeper, still facing him), slowed up, steadied himself—and then crashed an unstoppable shot into the back of the net. It was Kevin himself who went to retrieve the ball before dashing back to the centre, punching the air with his free hand. Kevin's exuberance was always a joy to see and his colleagues gave him the hero's welcome he deserved.

Rainhurst never recovered from that double blow. They tried hard to salvage something from the match but they sensed it was not going to be their day. Only their goalkeeper, now recovered from his injury, covered himself with glory.

Twice before half-time he prevented what seemed like certain goals from Adrian Dawnay and Kevin with fearless dives at their feet. His courage ought to have inspired his team but the Rainhurst players weren't clever enough to contain the Town Boys' attacks.

Soon after the interval the rain ceased and the sun came out again. It seemed to act as a signal to the visiting forwards to renew their all-out assault on the home goal. Again and again they were thwarted by brilliant goalkeeping until, following another solo run by Kevin, the ball was side-footed into the net by Gary, whose pleasure at scoring matched his friend's. Five minutes later he repaid the compliment for Kevin to grab his second goal—and the last one of the tour.

Mr Gregsten congratulated each player individually as he came off the field at the end. The memory of the team's only defeat had now been rubbed out. The tour had ended in triumph.

"Well," he said, as the boys climbed into the coach for the long journey home, "I hope you've all enjoyed the experience of going on tour. We've had one or two disappointments, and one or two scares, but I think we've come out on top. Whatever else, you all know now what it's like playing away from home."